Coastal Midlife Magic

By

Brandi Wilde

This book or part thereof may **not** be reproduced in any form by any means, electronic or mechanical, including photocopy, recording, or otherwise, or by any information storage and retrieval system, except as may be expressly permitted in writing from the publisher as provided by the United States of America copyright law. Requests for permission should be addressed to Swallowtail Productions, LLC, Attn: Rights and Permissions Dept., PO Box 536, Lewiston, ID   83501-0536.

Warning: The unauthorized reproduction or distribution of this copyrighted work is illegal. Criminal copyright infringement, *including infringement without monetary gain*, is investigated by the FBI and **is punishable by up to 5 years in federal prison and/or a fine of $250,000**. (See http://www.fbi.gov/ipr/ for more information about intellectual property rights.) This book is a work of fiction and any resemblance to persons living or dead, or places, events, or locales is purely accidental. The characters are reproductions of the author's imagination and used fictitiously.

* * * * *

Note to readers: I have changed the spelling of the name for Dantelion to: *Danteleon* to make it easier to pronounce. To pronounce Rafe's name, it rhymes with safe. I hope this helps all of you.

- 8 -

Dedication

This book is dedicated to those authors whose books I've read that have inspired my muse to go off on a tangent into the magickal paranormal world of witches, shifters, and demons.

Without readers, my stories would have no home, so I also dedicate this book to those of you who continue to support Indie authors. You are who keep us writing and my characters thank each and every one of you.

I want to thank those in the investigation and law enforcement field for your help in making the story details factually correct. Thank you to my editors and proofreaders who make my work readable for the public. Without your dedication to finding mistakes, my work would be meaningless. I appreciate you.

I also dedicate this book to my husband, John, who has put up with my *multiple personalities* over the years of my writing career. He humors me and makes me laugh, not to mention, he's also helped with the police technicalities of this book. Thank you for being there for me.

I also want to thank my friends who understood when I had to decline an invitation because I needed to get writing, edits, or newsletters done. All of you stand behind my creative side and you understand.

Chapter 1

As Kinsley rode her Harley hell-bent for home, she breathed in the ocean air as she headed north along Highway 101. She had to release the anger that swelled up like a tsunami after seeing Kai inside the Dragon's Lair. *Just where the hell did he come from and what brought him to the west coast?* She barely noticed the cars that passed her on her way up to Pebble Cove, but when a patrol car goes by…one notices.

Shit! That patrol car could only belong to one person.

Rafe. And it looked like Nate in the car with him.

She sped up, needing to ignore that fact, for a moment, yet she wondered why *he* was going in the direction of the Dragon's Lair. Maybe he needed to discuss something with Diablo. Not her worry. Kai was her worry right now. Why, after all these years, would she run into him in the middle of nowhere? It was too much just to be a coincidence.

Hardly!

Concentrate on getting home safe!

Clear your head and don't get distracted while you ride.

The drive and fresh air did her good during the thirty-minute trip. She slowed her speed to pull in past her iron gates at her driveway and up the gravel path to the garage. Only when she parked inside, and got off the bike, did she allow herself to rethink her meeting with Kai and the angry memories those blue eyes had created.

Kinsley hung her helmet on the handlebars and went into the mudroom. The house was silent. Angela must be working late at her shop. She looked around, then headed up to her room, still stewing from her contact with Kai and the massive internal storm he'd created. Stomping up the steps helped her push out her body's pent-up stress.

When she glanced up, her ferret, Gibbs, sat at the top of the stairs shaking his head. He'd been her familiar for a few years now and he still snuck up on her. Occasionally, his advice *did* make sense, and he always cheered her up.

"You could wake up the dead with all that stomping around. Teleporting up here would be way quieter for those of us trying to catch a few winks." He rubbed at his eyes with his tiny paws. "What could be so earth-shattering that you need to make so much noise?"

She rubbed his small head and tweaked his ear. "If you only knew! And why are you sleeping this late in the afternoon when you should be out hunting?" Kinsley stepped around him on the way to her room.

Gibbs scampered after her. "When I get gourmet meals here, why should I waste my time out there?"

"You might gather information from the trees or the flowers, right?"

"All they chat about are the murders, yet none of them have seen who's doing it." Gibbs jumped up to grip onto a pair of jeans and climbed her clothes tree to balance on top so he could continue his conversation.

She hung up her leathers without bumping Gibbs and changed into shorts and a tank top.

"Would you like a ride downstairs?" Kinsley held out her arm and he jumped on. She snuggled him close so she wouldn't drop him and headed to her bar downstairs. Another double whiskey and a trip outside to the screen room would help her think.

Maybe too much.

Gibbs tiny claws dug into her arm as he held on. "If I had magick to teleport, I sure wouldn't be wasting my time traipsing down these stairs, so don't drop me!"

"It's a good thing you don't have magick abilities. Goddess knows we'd be in a heap of trouble!" At the bottom landing, Gibbs leapt from her arm onto the back of a chair and scampered toward the bar.

With a drink in hand, she went out to sit in the cushioned wicker chair and put her feet up. She moved a pillow onto her lap for Gibbs and he took his spot so he could see into the yard. Dusk was settling in and the fog over the ocean appeared thicker. Kinsley sipped at her drink, swirled it over her tongue, and let the bite of her whiskey mellow out.

She thought back on sitting at the bar in the Dragon's Lair. The moment she looked up into the mirror and saw those icy blue eyes gaze back at her in recognition, her heart felt ripped from her chest one more time.

Her grip tightened on her glass.

Just when she thought she might be getting over the man, he had the nerve to show his face in her neighborhood. His longer, silky blonde hair looked good on him, as much as she hated admitting it. She didn't want to think more about him just when she and Rafe were moving forward with their relationship.

Now her feelings were all over the place instead of down one path. The memories flooded back of their years together in high school. His tender kisses. His strong arms that had made her feel protected. Those same eyes that she'd gotten lost in too many times.

A warm tear slipped down her cheek, surprising her that he could make her cry after so many years. Gibbs noticed and crawled up her shirt front to cuddle around her neck. He always seemed to know when she needed that. Glad that she was alone, she let the tears fall and allowed her heart to break yet again. How many times would she let a man tear her apart? Too many years had passed for this to be happening and make her cry over a past that was long gone and over.

Did he even think of her like that today?

She reached for a tissue and dried her face and nose, took a long drink, then took a deep breath.

He can't break your heart unless you let him! Straighten up!

Rafe is willing to accept that she had loved before and still wanted a future with her...if she'd allow it.

Wanting to slam her glass on the cement floor would solve nothing except to create a mess. Like the shards of her heart, the glass would shatter into a million pieces. She squeezed her eyes tight and ran her hand over Gibbs' back.

Why?

Goddess, she wanted to forget him!

Then she remembered those long fingers that had reached out to caress her neck as he went behind her this afternoon. She'd stopped him and shocked him at the same time. At least he pulled away, but he was too quick for her and caught her foot just as she was aiming her boot for the family jewels. Their past relationship hadn't involved those. He'd respected her when she said no. Now she wished she'd made a different choice. Had she said yes to sex back then, she could have been raising a child alone. She doubted he would have stuck around.

Water under the bridge.

But damn, they would have been good together.

Kinsley laid her head back to rest but visions of icy blue eyes haunted the darkness. Gibbs' cold little nose nudged behind her ear for comfort.

Half an hour later, the back door opened, and she heard Angela come in.

"I'm out here!" Kinsley hoped her face wouldn't give her away. She didn't want to rehash seeing Kai right now. Angela knew about Kai but not about how deep her feelings went. Only Destiny knew her that well. One day, maybe she'd give her a call and let her know she'd run into Kai, but she wasn't ready for that step yet.

Angela stepped in front of her with the opened whiskey bottle she'd left on the counter. "Bad day? Need a refill?"

Kinsley held out her glass of melting ice. "*I* don't but fill it up for Gibbs!" Fresh golden courage half-filled her glass.

"Care to talk about it? You and Rafe okay?"

"Yes, we're fine. Just a shitty day. It'll pass."

"Let me grab some wine. I'll be right back."

Gibbs popped up his head. "I'm outta here! Not good to be around when the magick clashes. See you later!" He pushed his little pet door open and outside he scampered.

Angela returned with a white wine and sat in the wicker chair beside her. "I had stock to sort out tonight. At least I won't have to do it tomorrow. I've got herbs and basil water to get prepared so we can ward Nate's place for Morgan on Friday. You going to join us?"

"Of course. Those two deserve to be happy without the threat of evil outsiders. It'll be good to get that completed for them. Thanks for warding Rafe's place with me. Now I can spend the weekends there without any worry."

Kinsley didn't want to think about that right now, even though Rafe was waiting for an answer about her staying this weekend. He did give her grounding and her feelings for him were just settling into place.

Kai's appearance at the bar had screwed all of that up!

Angela's wine glass vibrated on the end table. "Umm, your thoughts are vibrating the whole house, hon. You're not okay. I don't care what you say."

Kinsley glanced over at Angela. "Sorry. I'm glad you're here with me. It's nice to have someone around. There's just a lot going on at the office, I guess. The surrounding towns are still complaining about the tourism numbers being down. I wish that killer would have chosen another area for their organ harvesting."

"Rafe hasn't found another body, has he?"

"Not that I know of, but three bodies are three too many. He said something about a forensics expert that might find something they've missed. I just want it over." Kinsley set her glass down and checked her phone. It wasn't like her to be home nearly an hour and not check for calls.

Rafe had left her a text message. *Hoping you're okay. You didn't answer your phone.*

She texted back that she was fine. Would he ask why she was in Hag Stone Cove? She'd hoped Diablo hadn't said anything to him about her and Kai. He usually kept things to himself, but she'd know soon enough if Diablo had spilled the beans. Surely Rafe would say something if he'd heard.

* * * * *

Morgan woke up with Nate's arm around her waist as she lay on her side. She still couldn't believe that her life had taken on such a magickal tone. Her universe was coming together as well as her abilities. She just needed to trust them. As she glanced at the window, the morning sun peeked through the blinds. Soon she would be living at Nate's place, and their future would be wonderful.

Warm lips touched her skin as Nate kissed her cheek and Morgan stretched within his arms. His hand flattened on her stomach and caressed its way up to cup her breast. "Morning, beautiful."

She wiggled her hips against his hardness on purpose, knowing what it did to him, and she wasn't disappointed. The full length of him pressed against her ass. "You still have energy left after last night?"

"I'll never run out of energy where you're concerned, babe."

His tongue teased the side of her neck, sending a shiver down her spine, remembering how she'd nearly made him shift during their lovemaking last night. Never in her life had a man made her feel as precious as Nate did. Life's future for them would be filled with happiness and she looked forward to each new day with him. "I can't wait to wake up with you every morning in our bed at your home. I love our life."

"That sounds promising, but I want the wards up before we take a chance on moving you in there. And we will move you slowly to be sure that's what you truly want to do. We're not in a rush to get you moved."

"Angela has everything ready. I think our plan is for tomorrow to get it done. Is that too soon for you?"

"Yesterday would not have been too soon. The place needs a woman's touch, and you have free reign to do as you please, with magick or not." Nate gave her a squeeze. "I need to head to the station. Rafe is interviewing the detective that his friend recommended. Not sure where he's from, but it should be interesting to see if he can figure out something about these murders that we haven't found. I'm off to the shower." He tossed back the covers and gave her ass a sharp slap. "That's to keep you warm all day!"

She yelped. It would do more than keep her warm. Her thoughts would be on sex all day. Nate walked out of the bedroom to the shower stark naked and she enjoyed the sexy view of his muscled body. *How had she fallen into this wonderful relationship?*

Morgan donned her robe and went out to get the coffee going so Nate could enjoy a cup on his way to the station. She thought about living at his place, then wondered if Izzy would still visit her there. The woman could certainly come and go as she pleased, so a new location shouldn't change her appearing wherever she wanted.

They'd not been to Nate's place often since the wards weren't up yet and getting that done was at the top of her priority list. It didn't matter whether Logan wanted this apartment or not, the place would stay the way it was. She'd not rent it out to anyone else until she was sure she wouldn't be returning.

Tomorrow would be warding day at Nate's, and she hadn't packed anything yet. *Am I ready to make that type of a move?* She wasn't sure about giving up her apartment and her independence, but life was different now than it had been when she was married to her ex-husband. Logan had seen the change and only wanted to be sure she was happy with Nate. She shuddered to think what Logan could do to Nate if shit went sideways. He'd slammed his own father up against a wall with just a thought and a nod of his head. Logan had never shown signs of magick before and he was probably as shocked as she was. The two hadn't talked much about it since it happened.

Nate startled her thoughts with a hug and Morgan smiled. The scent of soap wafted around them with a hint of his cologne. She rubbed the strong arms that held her, feeling his muscles move beneath her fingers. Muscles that loved her touch. Yes, she was happy and making the right decisions.

His lips seared up the side of her neck. "I love waking up with you." He reached up into the cupboard for his travel mug and she filled it. "I'll call you later, babe. Have a good day with Logan. I think you two need to read through the grimoire soon. Especially if Jadis will be here in a few days to begin his training."

She walked him to the door. "You're right. We can't afford to put that off. He needs to learn as much information as we can get crammed in. I'm afraid for his future if my visions are correct. He has so much to learn and so little time."

"The two of you will figure it out. Neither of you are alone in this. You have all of us." With that, he left, and she knew he would be sure the downstairs door locked her in.

As she grabbed a coffee for herself, the air rippled around her and Izzy appeared in her chair with a full teacup. "Good morning, my dear."

Morgan laughed. "I appreciate that you wait until he's gone to show up!"

"I'm not so crass as to show up at inopportune times. I would never do that."

The old woman had her gray hair done up on top of her head with dark purple ribbons today and a dress that matched. Then again, Izzy was always tidy and sharp. "Did you dress up for a special occasion today?"

"No, but I did want to dress up for others who may have seen me down in the bookstore. Logan does such a wonderful job. He's already protecting you. That was quite the show with your ex-husband the other day."

"Yes, it was. I assumed you would know about it."

"I did. Oh, Jadis is arriving later today, just so you know. She's coming to the store."

Morgan stared at the old woman as she went over to sit on the sofa with her coffee. "Thank you for the heads up. No one has bothered to inform me otherwise. Wow. My parents only said she'd arrive in a few days." She was curious about this *woman.* Would she look younger or older? Morgan envisioned a woman as old as Izzy trying to train her son in the art of combat. She couldn't wait to find out.

"You aren't using your psychic abilities to their fullest. I'm just going to say that you need to *own* that ability. You'll appreciate it more. I'm just sayin'." Izzy giggled.

"Does it have to do with this woman coming into town?"

"Now if I told you everything, what good would that do? You need to see the visions to understand the repercussions." Izzy raised a brow as she sipped. "Do you have your own scrying mirror yet? Suzie might be able to help you with that. You should go visit her."

Morgan gasped. "You tell me just enough to cause trouble, don't you?" She pressed her head back against the sofa and rolled her eyes. "Just tell me already!"

"You're going to have a wonderful week, my dear." Izzy set her teacup on the saucer and faded away.

Do I need to visit Suzie at her antique shop?

Chapter 2

With a snap of her fingers, Morgan changed and readied herself for the day. Then she placed her palms on the kitchen counter, calmed herself and grounded her feet as she closed her eyes. Behind her lids the darkness turned into light as a dark-haired woman came into view with a ponytail, dressed in a tie-dyed shirt, large round sunglasses, and jeans.

A hippie from back in the day?

Morgan nearly laughed out loud. Who was her father sending to train Logan?

Yes! I need to visit Suzie today and see if she has any black mirrors.

Morgan locked her apartment door and made her way down to the bookstore. A raspberry latte would start her day off right. As she headed toward the coffee shop, Logan was deep in conversation with a woman wearing a tie-dyed shirt and a ponytail. Her large, rimmed sunglasses rested on top of her head.

As she got closer, Morgan took in a deep breath. The woman stood as tall as Logan's shoulders and still shorter than herself.

When she approached, Logan looked up and smiled. "Hi, mom! I'll get your latte going. This is Jadis. She just got into town."

The woman was stunning with green eyes, dark hair and contoured muscles in her arms and legs. She appeared to be about forty, but Morgan knew she was at least as old as her parents. *I sure as hell hope I look that good when I'm over one hundred years old!* "I've been looking forward to meeting you. My father said you are more than qualified to help Logan with his abilities." She shook the manicured hand Jadis had extended to her. Naturally, the woman had a firm grip.

"I understand we need to move quickly as a spell will wear off soon with this demon. I know of him, and he's ruthless when he sets his sights on those out of his reach. I will be in town a few weeks, maybe longer, until I'm sure Logan can handle himself without me around."

Logan passed Morgan her coffee as he looked at Jadis. "What type of training are we talking about? Gym workouts, agility training, magick…which I still have my doubts that I even possess."

Jadis gave Logan a look that took in the entire length of his body until he shifted his weight under her perusal. Then she glanced at Morgan before looking back at Logan. "I'm pretty good at sensing the power of others and you are way at the top of that chart, son. Make no mistake. You *have* abilities and then some. My job is to make sure you're aware of how best to use them to your benefit against any enemies." She met Morgan's gaze. "I hear the family grimoire is in your possession, correct?"

"It is. The three of us can meet upstairs later and go through it. There are many pages neither of us have gotten to."

Jadis took a drink of her coffee. "It's imperative we make sure you both learn the family history and what a protector does." She finished her drink and tossed the cup in the wastebasket. "I want to check out the gym facilities. It'll be easier to work down there on the weight benches so his body strength can gain superiority." Jadis gave her card to both

Logan and Morgan. "Please send me a text so that I have both of your numbers. I want to start tomorrow at the gym with Logan."

"Sounds great. I'll meet you there tomorrow." Logan watched the sway of the woman's hips as she walked out of the store.

Morgan tapped his chin, and he blinked, making her laugh. "Keep those thoughts separate from your training, son. That woman is older than she appears!" She laughed over her shoulder on her way out the door. "I'll be back later. I'm going down to talk with Suzie at her shop."

Shaking her head, Morgan's thoughts swirled through her head about Logan's attention span with a beautiful female trainer. His hormones would get the best of him if he wasn't careful. The boy was quickly growing into a man, and as his mother, she'd have to try hard not to stick her nose into his business.

At Suzie's shop, Morgan looked around as she conversed with Suzie. "I need to get a scrying mirror, and I'd like it to be a black one with fancy ornate framing. One that I can set on a table."

Suzie scanned the area of shelves where she kept most of her mirrors. "I know I have two back here that are black mirrors. You can pick from them." She carefully took the mirrors over to a table where she had for customers to use.

"Those are beautiful!" Morgan sat down and pulled both over to her. She let her fingers caress the frames as she closed her eyes and concentrated to know which one would speak to her. When the mirror in her right hand warmed her fingers, visions formed in her mind, and she immediately opened her eyes. She laid the mirror on the left face down. In the glass on the right, a misty swirl of silver and blues tried to form a vision but immediately went black.

Morgan sighed and met Suzie's gaze. "I think this one is trying to speak to me. I'll take this one." Her fingertips touched the ornate swirling black filament on the frame and traced the small gargoyle head on each corner. "Is it normal for a mirror to react to its owner like this?"

A smile covered Suzie's lips. "It is. If you can feel it, then that's the one for you. Our intuition is never wrong. You need to trust yourself, hon. Should I package it up for you?"

"Yes. I'm happy I found one so fast, thank you. I knew you'd have what I needed. Hey, are you helping us ward Nate's place tomorrow? I can't wait to get that done so we won't have to worry about *him* anymore."

"I will be there to help. All of us are happy that you and Nate are together. If you need help packing, let us know."

* * * * *

Rafe met Nate in the small conference room and laid the files on the table. "I hope this guy knows what he's up against. This case needs a break. I'm not so sure he can find something we've overlooked but who knows."

Trish tapped on the doorframe of the conference room. "Sheriff? This is Mr. McGarrett. I'll bring in more coffee."

Same as the first time he met Kai at the Dragon's Lair, Rafe sensed the man went deeper than his outward appearance. His background was Special Forces Night Stalker, and Rafe's friend, Michael, had said he was one of the best. His blond hair was no longer high and tight, as it must have been in the military, but touched his collar and covered the top of his ears. His broad shoulders spoke of the strength of the man, and he obviously worked out on a daily basis. The icy blue of his eyes were a color Rafe hadn't seen often, and appeared as though they could pierce a sheet of steel.

"Thank you, Trish. Come on in, Kai. We're both glad you could join us. Michael gave you a great reference and said you're the best we could get. I've brought in the files we're working on for your review. We've got three bodies so far, not any of them in good condition when we found them and internal organs were missing from each victim."

Kai raised a brow. "Exactly what organs were missing?"

"Hearts, livers, lungs, pancreas, just to list a few." Rafe explained what had happened with each discovery so far to fill Kai in on what had been done. Kai asked questions, wrote down notes, drank his coffee with cream, and didn't snack much. He couldn't help but feel respect for a man with his background.

After an hour of intense discussion, Rafe pushed his coffee away. "Let's get the obvious out of the way. We're all shifters here, and my pack members have been doing patrols. They all know you'll be in town. It won't take them long to figure out you're also a shifter, if they haven't already. We have a few troublemakers, and they were in the Dragon's Lair when you were there."

"I sensed them before I even walked in the door."

"We're wolves, Diablo at the bar, and his woman, are bear shifters. I'm not sure what you are."

Kai tipped his head up and leveled his blue gaze on Rafe. "I've been a cougar shifter since I was twenty-one. It came in handy on many cases I've worked on, and it goes without saying how handy it was during our night-time recon assignments in the military. This case will be the same. If it's necessary, I will shift for tracking. Being a cougar gives me the ability to climb trees if needed. Do you have any suspects at this point? Everything shows no evidence had been found on any of the bodies. And who is the coroner to you?"

Rafe laid his pen down. "He's been a friend for years. His name is Dexter Grissom, and he's pretty thorough. He's as stumped as we are with no evidence. He verified the precise cuts used to remove all of the internal organs."

Kai finished his coffee. "It appears to me the suspect not only wore gloves, but a hazmat suit that covered their entire body, so nothing gets left behind. From the coroner's notes, it appears the perp could be right-handed. Have any cell tower records been pulled?"

"Shit, no." Rafe looked at Nate. "Get warrants ordered before you leave today so we can get those delivered to the companies."

Nate raised a brow and looked at Kai. "We also have a cell phone packed in silicone to dry it out."

Rafe leaned forward. "Guessing it was a burner phone, but we do have the sim card intact. Not sure if anything can be pulled from it since it was found in shallow water."

"I have access to special software. We might get lucky and pull something off." Kai nodded as he scanned through the files. "Regarding the missing organs, do you know people at any of the nearby transplant centers? If we check with them, maybe they've had an abundance of body parts lately."

Rafe made his own notes. "I may have a contact there we can reach out to. I'll check on that. Somehow, the organs are getting out to a pickup person right away. By air or water, we have no clue at this point. No footprints have been found at any of the crime scenes."

"Maybe by watercraft. I'd like to talk with the boat captain who found the body in the water. Do you know him well?"

Nate spoke up. "He's been here a few years; he came from California. Previous surfer dude who now has more interest in charter fishing. The first thing we saw when we went to his place of business were the knives he kept on a magnetic strip above his fishing table. It's quite a collection. At the moment, he was not a suspect."

"So, he owns the boats at the marina next to the cabins. I checked into one. Maybe I'll roam over and talk with him for a few minutes. He doesn't need to know who I am right away. I'll see what I can come up with." Kai made a few more notes of his own, closed the files, and pushed them back toward Rafe. "I'd like to talk with the coroner, too, if you don't mind, and his assistant. Just to tick off a few points in my head."

Rafe jotted down the coroner's number. "I'll let him know you'll be calling. I hope you can find something we've missed. These cases are adding up too fast, and it's not good for the communities. The people want this killer caught."

Kai stood to push in his chair. "I'll get some nighttime searches done this weekend and go over the areas where the bodies were dumped. Not that you guys missed anything, but another pair of eyes can't hurt. We can work on the cell phone Monday with my software to see what's on the sim card. I'll keep you posted and check in on Monday."

Rafe and Nate walked to the door with Kai. "We can use all the help we can get. There has to be something we missed." Kai left the office, and Rafe shook his head. "I didn't want to like the guy, but I do, and I think he can help us."

"Is it a good idea to have him prowling the woods? We need to alert the pack so they know not to attack a cougar if they see one."

"Good point. Let them know. I'm going over to check on Kinsley at her office. Don't forget to call in for those warrants so we can get the records from the cell towers."

Rafe stopped at the doorway. "Hey, isn't the coven putting up wards at your place tomorrow tonight? That should help out a lot so that Morgan isn't in danger when she's there. At least not from *outside* evil! I'm not so sure about danger lurking *inside* your home between you two!"

"Funny, asshole!" Nate rolled his eyes and picked up his phone as Rafe closed the door.

In the truck, Rafe texted Kinsley before he headed over to her office. He wouldn't get to spend time with her tomorrow night until after the warding got completed at Nate's place. At least she would be safe there. Nate would feel better, too, once they knew the demon couldn't wreak havoc on his property.

His packmate had done well for himself. Nate's home was a brick one-story home with two end-wings, one off each end of the main home; one was the main wing for him and Morgan and the other had guest bedrooms with on-suites, all overlooking a built-in pool with a hot tub, much like his own backyard. A view of the ocean could be seen from both of their homes.

* * * * *

Friday evening, Kinsley worked with Angela as they gathered the rosemary, oak leaves and acorns, her salt mixture, and agrimony. Basil water was needed to set the wards at Nate's home. Before they started, both washed their hands in rosemary water to cleanse away any spiritual attachments.

Angela then set the herbs on the kitchen counter in baskets. She held up a large jar of her salt mixture. "I love this! The salt, ground together with acorns and thorns from rosebushes and Hawthorne trees, gives great protection against evil. I've ground up pine needles to sprinkle over the property outside. If any herbs are left over, I'll give them to Morgan for her herb room."

Kinsley double checked the supplies as she always did. The two had agreed to double-check like that when they first began to organize things so nothing was forgotten.

"Here are extra bottles of basil water and bundles of rosemary for Morgan to keep at the house. She's going to have so much fun setting up her herb room at Nate's. I can't wait to see his place." Angela set the bottle and sprayers in another basket.

"Morgan said to be there by six, so we better get going. We only have a week left of the thirty-day limit her father cast on Danteleon's powers. Who knows what he will be capable of once he regains his full-blown abilities. He certainly is going to be on a revenge mission. Let's load up my car and head over."

Kinsley grabbed three baskets and went to the garage to pack the back of her Yukon. Angela followed with the remaining items. "I'll be glad once this is done, and we won't have to worry so much about *him* getting at Morgan. This ward and shield will do the trick to stop him." She climbed into the driver's seat and drove to Nate's home.

The short drive to Nate's home got them there just as the other coven members were parking. Morgan and Nate were outside greeting them and Kinsley backed in to unload. She hugged Morgan, then handed her some baskets to take inside.

Morgan set the baskets on the huge island in the kitchen. "Nate and I gathered the four small boulders from the edge of his property like Angela asked."

"Good! I have the herbs and stones so we can bless them, so they understand what is expected of them when we bury them in each corner of your property." Angela pulled out the herbs and black salt, along with the sage bundles. "Once we sage the inside, every corner of every room, we'll use the remaining ashes to cover the stones after we oil them."

"I've dug the four holes at each corner also." Nate stood anxiously waiting next to Morgan. "Thank you, ladies, for taking the time to protect our home for us. I'll be more comfortable when Morgan is here knowing the ward is up and working."

"Let's get started." Angela lit six white candles. Each of them paused as she prayed for peace and grounding before they began. Then she passed out bundles to Suzy, Jenna, Kinsley, Margo, Katie, and Morgan, along with a feather and large clam shells for the bundle to rest in once it started smoking. "Nate, you can walk through the rooms in your wing with Morgan. She knows the prayer to say while she spreads the smoke throughout. Any questions?"

They spread out and began the smudging. Kinsley did the large living room of the open floor plan, and Angela worked in the kitchen. "We call upon the benevolent spirits of earth, air, fire, and water. Please remove any evil and unwelcome spirits. May no harm come to those who dwell here. Only positive love and energy are welcome." They both repeated this for every corner of every room.

When they all gathered back in the kitchen, Angela poured the sage ashes over the black salt in her dish, and crushed Hawthorne and ground rose thorns among the salt and ashes and mixed them together. "This mixture will be sprinkled at the corners of the home before we bury each boulder. When we place the boulder, it will be sprinkled with my oils, then sprinkled with this mixture. As we bury each stone, we will connect the ward to the boulder for stronger protection. Every thirty days, sprinkle basil water over each one that is buried. You will both be safe on your property. We love you both." She let Morgan carry the salt ash and Kinsley took the specially prepared oil and they proceeded outside.

The procedure amazed Nate. The prayers and procedures were precise for protecting his home so his woman would be safe. Burying and blessing the stones took about an hour. Once all was completed, the women returned to the kitchen. Morgan got wine glasses out for all of them and Nate grabbed his dark beer. "We can't thank you enough for all you've done. Please know we appreciate each of you. Thank you."

Kinsley checked her phone. "Rafe is on his way. I hope that is okay."

"Of course. I'm glad he's coming over." Morgan stepped close to Nate, and he put his arm around her shoulder as she looked up at him with her beautiful smile. "Now I can be here with you like we planned. This is wonderful."

"I'm glad I could join in for this, but I have to get back to the restaurant and relieve Mandy. She's amazing at holding down the business while I'm gone, but I think she has plans with

Logan tonight." Katie, who owned *Krazy Locals Cafe*, finished her wine and scurried out the door.

Margo, who owned *Magick Knots Bakery*, set a small white box on the counter with a beautiful purple bow and ribbon. "This is just a little something for the two of you to make your first night here a memorable one. You can't open it until you're alone together. Sorry. A little anticipation never hurts. I sell these at the bakery." Margo gave Nate a cute wink.

Nate leaned over and sniffed the box, then winked at Morgan. "I smell chocolate and strawberries!"

"That's cheating, Nate!" Kinsley pulled the box over to her side of the island as everyone joined in the laughter.

Margo made her excuses and left with Jenna, who owned the beach cabins, and Suzy, who owned *Antiques with AfterLife.*

Chapter 3

Rafe arrived as they were leaving. "Am I missing the party?"

Kinsley met him and gave him a quick kiss. "The celebration is just beginning. Everyone is now safe from the evil and it will stay that way. Angela can drive my car home later and I can go home with you, hon."

She winked at Rafe and Nate felt happy for the two of them. The wards had been placed on his home so Kinsley would be safe going there. He glanced at Morgan as he handed a beer to Rafe. "So...what decorating ideas do you have in mind to make yourself comfortable here? The choices are yours, babe. This is your home now, too."

She turned to look around the kitchen and into the living room. "A few pictures would make it cozy. Maybe a soft blanket on the sofa. But as long as I'm with you, I'll be at home here."

Nate loved the excitement in her eyes. He couldn't believe that he'd finally found a woman who melted the walls around his heart. Nate pulled her close. "Everything is white. I didn't pay attention to color when I moved in. So, we can talk about it." He tipped his beer for a drink. "Should we move this party to the patio? There's a beautiful sunset out back."

Nate couldn't have been happier to finally have Morgan at his side, and friends over to share in their time together. He looked forward to waking up with Morgan each day and going to sleep with her every night. Her needs would be taken care of, and he wanted his home comfortable so she could feel at ease here.

Once they were seated, Morgan cuddled closer. He just wished the gloom and doom at the back of his mind would disappear. It related to his past when he'd lost his first wife; they had been so happy. His heart hadn't healed for years after that and even now, fear ate at him to completely let go and just enjoy the moments he shared with Morgan.

She nudged his side with her shoulder and whispered up at him. "Are you okay, babe? Are you sure this is what you want?"

Her eyes glistened and nearly broke his heart. Tears began to pool in her eyes, and he didn't want her to feel that way. His thumb tenderly wiped away a tear that had escaped and now he felt like an ass. "Of course this is what I want. I've wanted this since the day I met you. Even though *you* didn't realize it, *I* did." He kissed her forehead. "I'm more than glad that you're here."

An hour later, Angela made her excuse to leave, and Kinsley gave her the keys to her Tahoe. "Drive careful, hon."

Nate retrieved more drinks for the four of them with Rafe's help. Once they were back at the poolside, he pushed the two double loungers closer so the four could talk and each couple cozied together. The warm evening breeze blew in the scent of the nearby pine trees and Nate relaxed knowing his wolf hadn't sensed any trouble around his home.

Kinsley held up her wine glass, tapped Rafe's can and then held it toward Nate and Morgan. "Here's to years of happiness for both of you. Morgan, Angela is anxious to help you set up your herb room. She's drying several for you now. You just need containers and bottles."

"I'd love her help and more knowledge on what each one does. Again, since my mother didn't teach me about the herbs and magick, I'm so in the dark I can't stand it."

"I'll be sure to let her know." Kinsley sipped her wine. "I'm glad Angela decided to move in with me a few years ago. We get along great."

Nate noticed the clouds circling overheard and the ocean waves slammed more violently against the rocks below. When lightning shot across the sky, Morgan sat up straight. She stared at Kinsley with wide eyes. "It's *him* again!"

Kinsley held out her hand as if to stop her worry. "The wards are in place. We have nothing to worry about. When we leave, we'll teleport to Rafe's to keep us safe."

"I can't stand the constant threat he seems to impose on us!"

Nate held Morgan closer. He hated that she was so afraid of the dark warlock, but she had good reason to be. "Would you rather we go inside and avoid the show he insists on creating?"

"I would. He ruins our view and intends to distract us. We're only safe from him for a few more days before he can begin again." She touched the necklace her mother had given her. "I'm glad that Logan has his ring to keep him safe."

Back in the kitchen, Kinsley sat her empty glass on the island. "I'm glad Jadis has arrived to begin Logan's training. Both of you will learn more about protecting yourselves and the powers you can use against him. I hope your father hears from the council soon to get him back behind bars that will hold him this time."

Rafe tossed his can in the recycle bin. "My pack is always available should any of you need us, Logan included. I look forward to watching his progress."

"He's meeting with her at the gym in the morning. I told him I'd open the coffee shop for him while he works with her. I won't lie...I was a little shocked when I met her. I'd envisioned an elderly person trying to train Logan. She looks to be 35, but we know she's as old as my parents, if not more so."

"I'm sure she'll teach both of you what your parents should have. The grimoire is filled with spells that you'll learn in time to help." Kinsley stepped over to put her arm around Rafe's waist. "Are you ready to head over to your place? I'm sure these two have lots to discuss. Hey, enjoy those chocolate-covered strawberries." She laughed as she winked at Morgan. "Call me if you need anything. We'll be in touch."

Nate watched the two as they disappeared before his eyes. He'd never get used to that form of travel, but it was safer that way. He glanced out the patio door as the lightning continued to strike the skies, caused by the demon warlock, and he checked the door lock, then pulled the curtain closed. With a shake of his head, he laughed at himself, as if closing the curtains would keep out a witch or demon.

When he glanced toward the kitchen island, Morgan watched him intently. He knew the demon scared her. He'd do his best to make sure she studied the grimoire and learned what she could to improve her powers. One day, she would be more powerful than this demon would want to tangle with.

He dimmed the lights, stepped closer, and wrapped his arms around her. She hugged him and spread her warm fingers over his back. The scent of her filled his lungs and touched every fiber of his body as he fought to keep his claws in. This woman healed him without even knowing it. "Should we open the gift that Margo brought?"

Morgan leaned back in his arms and looked up at him, her eyes begging him to take her right here in the kitchen. "I think we should. They smell wonderful." She tugged at the ribbon of the bow and pulled it away, then opened the box.

Nate leaned closer. Delicate, huge, red strawberries were covered in dark chocolate with white chocolate drizzled over them. He reached in to pull one out and held it to Morgan's lips. As she bit into it, her tongue darted out to catch the juices and his knees nearly buckled. Nate took in a quick breath as he watched her enjoy the sweetness.

She moaned as she chewed the decadent dessert, her fingers wiping at the juice that escaped her lips. "Oh, Nate. Wow." Her eyes rolled back in her head.

He gave her another bite of the chocolate and strawberry. It smelled so good, and he knew he'd have to stop by that bakery for more of these. When she held up his berry, he bit into it and the sweet, tart flavor exploded over his tongue. Her eyes met his and he hoped she caught on to the dreamy look he gave her. "Almost as sweet as you taste, babe. Should we take the other two into the bedroom?"

Morgan's teeth bit into her lower lip and that move alone made him hard where he stood. He set down the stem of the strawberry and cupped her face, his thumbs caressing her cheeks as he memorized her lips before kissing them. Her arms circled his waist, and he pressed her against the island with his hips. She tasted of chocolate and sweet strawberries. Nate swept her tongue with his and pulled from the kiss.

He rested his forehead against hers and took in a deep breath to calm himself. This woman scattered his thoughts, and made his body react like some teenager. Once he was stable, he lifted her in his arms, anxious to make her first night in her new home one she wouldn't soon forget. "You might want to grab the box to take with us. You'll need the nourishment. I have plans for the rest of the night.

* * * * *

As Kai sat in the Adirondack chair, with his boots on the porch railing of the cabin facing the ocean, he listened to the night sounds. His thoughts were on the murders and how he could help. The lights from the marina twinkled in the distance. He wanted to talk with the captain. Perhaps he'd remember something he hadn't told Rafe or maybe a small memory of finding the body that he hadn't thought important at the time.

A wooded area was on his left and he saw lights in the cabin at the far end, but the other cabins in between were empty. Kai itched to take a walk on the beach to look around. For what, he wasn't sure, just a hunch at this point. There had to be a few clues the sheriff and his deputy had overlooked. He'd hate to go through all the trouble of investigating to find nothing, but that was rarely the case for those he'd worked on.

He went inside to change into a tee shirt and running shorts to make it easier when he transformed to his cougar shape, should that be necessary. Once he changed, he locked the door, slipped the key into his pocket, and zipped it. Warm sand gathered between his toes as he walked, the waves lightly washing it away with each step. The full moon lit up the waves and he found it peaceful out here.

The marina called to him, so he headed that way from the beach. When he got close enough, someone was washing down a boat, which he found odd after dark, although the lights were bright that he used onboard. Kai's first thought went to getting rid of blood from body parts but then laughed at himself. The man saw him coming and stood still on the deck of the forty-foot fishing boat.

"A bit late to be out washing the deck, isn't it?"

"I had a group out fishing late today. When you run fishing charters, one has to work when time allows. You're out late tonight, man. What's up, dude?" As he talked, he re-tied his long, wavy hair into a man-bun and Kai laughed to himself.

"I'm staying a few nights at the cabins and thought I'd take a stroll on the beach." Kai stepped up onto the docks and walked toward the boat.

"I'm Bryce. Charter Captain. I kind of love what I do, and I get to help people enjoy the love of deep-sea fishing. Nothing like being out on the ocean with no land for miles. Kinda peaceful."

Kai leaned on a railing near the boat. "Do you clean and fillet the fish when they come back in?"

"I do! A sharp blade makes it easy work. Let me know if you want to go out while you're here. I'd be happy to take you." Bryce continued to wipe down the boat walls and windows, then sprayed down the deck.

"Nice meeting you. If you have free time in two days, I'd be interested in talking about a trip."

"I got you, dude. I'll mark it down so I'm free. Talk to you then. I gotta finish this up. Another early run at dawn tomorrow." Bryce tossed his rag in the bucket and picked up the hose.

Kai let him finish and walked down the dock and up toward the main shed where the fish cleaning likely took place. The door was wide open, so he stepped inside to look around and instantly saw the knives on a magnetic strip along the wall. Kai moved closer to check out the blades. Quite a collection of fillet knives...also used to slice and dice a human? One had to wonder as he examined them for signs of blood.

"They're all sharp as hell so be careful, man."

It was unusual for someone to walk up behind Kai, and he scolded himself for not watching his own back as he turned toward Bryce. "I bet they make your job easier. You wouldn't want to fillet a fish with a dull blade."

"Nope. I always keep them sharp. They make me money, so I can't be lax on that. I need to get my job done fast and right. I've been doing it long enough to be quick and good at it." Bryce watched him as Kai moved back toward the door.

"Quite the collection. It only goes without saying that you would need good blades. I'll let you close up shop. Talk to you in a few days." Kai walked back toward his cabin as he cataloged the conversation with Bryce, again scolding himself for not noticing when Bryce walked in. The man knew what he was doing but didn't appear to be a killer of humans, though he wouldn't cross Bryce off the list just yet.

* * * * *

Logan pulled into the parking lot of the gym bright and early to meet Jadis. He wondered what she could teach him and how it would help working out at the gym. He grabbed his gym bag and went inside so he'd be ready, but when he got inside, she'd beat him there. "Let me drop my bag in a locker. I'll be right there."

When he returned, he found Jadis sitting at a table near the smoothie counter and joined her. It would give him time to ask questions and figure out what her strategy would be to teach him magick at the gym. At this point, he was more than confused about all of it. He hadn't known he had abilities until a few weeks ago. What he'd read in the grimoire with his mom was confusing and like reading a faery tale.

She kicked out a chair for him and he sat down. "I know you're wondering what a workout at the gym has to do with your magick. We won't discuss much about that here where others can hear, but your future with this demon guy will depend on your strength and I don't plan on letting you fall behind in that department. Your grandfather has asked me to help, and I won't let him down. I want you running to build up your heart and lungs, and weight training to get your body strong enough to do physical fighting should it ever come to that. In the magickal world, none of us knows what the future may hold, but we must be ready. Does that make sense to you now?"

Logan nodded. It all made sense now that he thought along the lines of fighting the evil powers that threatened him and his mother. Thoughts of Mandy came to mind. One day he may have to fight a battle to protect her. His determination took a turn today with a new understanding of his future. "I realize that physically, I need to be ready, but how am I ever going to learn the magical abilities?"

"The wards are now in place at Nate's. I understand they did that the other night. That makes it safe for us to train in the backyard and away from prying eyes. I can put up the visibility shield should this dark warlock think to watch what you learn. At the same time, I'll teach both of you how to place them up also. We have much to learn and no time to waste."

Jadis sipped her water and watched him as she explained things to Logan. "I want you running daily and lifting weights for your arms, shoulders, and thighs. Your body will sense the change, and your abilities will help you get stronger. I want you to start today by always being aware of your surroundings. Tune into what is around you that you can see...and what you can't. Even though you can't see it, you'll sense danger without realizing it. That is part of the abilities you need to work on in your head."

Logan shouldn't be surprised at what he might one day be able to do, but it was all a bit overwhelming. He was proud to be learning from someone with as much knowledge as Jadis had. His grandfather would not have requested her help otherwise.

She was beautiful and kept herself in shape, and he noticed the other men in the gym watching them, mainly Jadis. His protective instincts kicked in as he looked around and gave them a warning look. One of them being a local firefighter who Logan didn't know well so he knew not to judge, but as long as he was near Jadis, he'd make sure she stayed safe.

"Are you ready to get started?"

"I am." With that, he stood up and she led the way to the weight bench. "I'm used to lifting so this will just be a refresher."

"I want you to continue adding weights weekly. You'll surprise yourself at how fast you become stronger. Make sure you're eating right."

Logan laid on the weight bench and began there, later moving to the thigh weights and triceps pull-downs, with Jadis instructing what he needed to do as she placed heavier weights on for him. The interested firefighter came by, and Logan tried not to listen to their small talk, but they were right next to him.

"Are you a new trainer here?" The man wiped his neck as he waited for her answer.

"Logan requested me. I do intense training...for those who are up to it." Jadis tightened the weight bolt, and Logan snickered to himself but held out his hand to the man.

"I'm Blake. You work at the coffee shop down in the bookstore, right?"

"I do." Logan redirected his attention back to lifting the new weight.

Jadis shook Blake's hand. "You don't look like you need any intense training." She gave him a smile as she made sure Logan didn't have trouble with what she'd loaded up for him.

Blake's gaze moved over her body and back to her eyes. "If you ever need help putting out that internal fire, I'll be around here now and then." Blake turned and left.

Jadis glanced his way as he walked toward the shower. "Nice tail, shifter!"

Logan happened to look at Blake in time to catch the narrowed gaze he gave Jadis. "I don't think he liked that. Why did you call him shifter?"

She shrugged a shoulder. "Firefighters always work different shifts at the station."

Her comment didn't make sense, but he ignored it. "I'll do five more lifts, and we can get a run in." He picked up the hand weights and slowly lifted as he counted. When he finished, he wiped down each hand weight and the machines he'd used. Logan led the way upstairs to the track on the second floor, and Jadis ran with him for thirty minutes. His mind thought of the grimoire that he knew he needed to read, front to back, so he understood what needed to be learned.

Thoughts of his future included Mandy, and he wanted to be there for her. Neither of them understood what they could do ability-wise. He wondered why he'd been chosen to be this *protector* person among the witch community. Logan had so many thoughts swimming in his head that he hadn't noticed Jadis had stopped running.

When he looked back, she was bent over with her hands on her knees, and he ran back to her. "Are you alright?"

She laughed. "I guess I need to pay more attention to my own training!"

"It's been a good start today. Thank you."

Jadis stood, her ponytail hanging down her back, and Logan again noticed that she only stood to his shoulders. "I think you know what you need to get done at the gym and how often. Tomorrow afternoon, we'll start training at

Nate's place in the backyard. I'll get the directions from your mom. She can join us. Both of you can discover your abilities at the same time. Hit the shower. I know you have to go back to help at the store. It was a good day."

Logan headed to the shower. When he got back to the store, Mandy was talking with his mom in the coffee shop. He sat down with them and squeezed Mandy's hand as he met her gaze. Her smile lit up her face and he knew he was lucky to be the one who caught her attention. "We had a good day at the gym. You're here early. Is everything okay?"

"It is. I just brought some cinnamon rolls by that my mom made. Your customers might like something different today. I won't keep you. I have to get back for the breakfast crowd at the restaurant."

"I'll walk you out." Logan held her hand until they got to her car out front. His thumb caressed the softness on the back of her hand. "I like Jadis. She pushes me to be better. I'm excited to learn what she can teach me. It all seems so unbelievable that any of this is even possible."

"I know. Since no one taught your mother that she had abilities, she couldn't help you like she should have. My mom hasn't taught me a lot, but she will now that we seem to be aware of an evil lurking in the community. She said we never had to deal with this before. It's all new to her and she can feel it, too."

"Sounds like all of us need training, huh? I'll see you later tonight?" Logan opened her door and watched for oncoming cars. It was still early morning and not many were out. "Mom is moving to Nate's, so the apartment upstairs will be a good place to read the family grimoire. I'm anxious to read more of it. You can join me."

"I'll text when I'm off work today. That sounds interesting. I'll bring a few sandwiches for us if that's okay."

"Good. I'll see you later. Please stay safe and pay attention to your surroundings and who might be following you. I don't trust this dark warlock. He better not even think to follow you because of me. I hate that this puts you in jeopardy." He squeezed her hand and then watched her drive away.

Back in the store, he mentioned to Morgan that he wanted to read upstairs tonight. "That sounds like a great idea, son."

"Mandy is coming over later with sandwiches. I hope it's okay if she reads with me."

"Of course. I need to get back to reading, too."

"Jadis wants to train in Nate's backyard tomorrow, if that's fine with you and Nate. She mentioned that you should join us. She'd like you to learn with me."

"I'm sure Nate won't care. It sounds like a great idea. I *will* join you two." When the bell on the door chimed, his mom went to greet the customer, and Logan made himself a coffee. He looked forward to seeing Mandy tonight. They needed more time alone together, and it never seemed to happen often enough with her helping her mom at the Krazy Local's restaurant.

Chapter 4

That morning at the sheriff's office, Kai sat with Rafe. He wanted to know the location of each body so he could visit just to scout out the area. Rafe marked on a makeshift map and showed where each body had been. "One was pulled from the water, one was found in the woods outside of Pebble Cove, and the other in the woods at Hag Stone. We have no idea where another body might be found, but I have no doubt there *will* be another body. I just don't like this at all."

"Pebble Cove sits between Hag Stone and Ravensville according to this. That gives me a lot of territory to cover. Pebble Cove also sits close to the California state line and Hag Stone nearly on the state line." Kai sat back, sipped his coffee and studied the location of open shorelines to each town. "Those organs could have been picked up anywhere along this coastline. Easy access to hospitals in either direction. Then there's the massive Redwood forest. Damn!"

"Bodies could be hidden anywhere, but I think the redwoods have too many people roaming around for our killer to want the attention he'd get down there. My guess would be between here and Ravensville. Just a hunch." Rafe pointed at the area on the hand-drawn map with his pencil.

Nate set a clear shoebox on the table filled with silica gel packets. "This is the phone that some kids found among rocks near the shore up the coast a bit. I hope you can pull something viable off this thing. It's just a burner phone so anything is possible."

Kai marked the spot on the map up the coast from Pebble Cove where the phone was found, then opened the box to get the phone parts out. "Do you have a cord handy to fit this so we can plug it in?"

Nate handed him the cord. "I matched it up when I put it away; knew we'd need one." He handed Kai a handful of papers. "These are the records from the cell towers. The numbers we need should be on there somewhere."

"Nice work, Nate. Thanks. We have to catch this guy." Rafe got up for more coffee and brought the pot back to refill Kai and Nate, then set the creamer on the table.

Kai put the phone back together and plugged the cord in, then placed his briefcase on the table and pulled out his laptop. Once it was up and running, he connected the phone cord to his device, tapped a program, and let it begin. While that was working, he took out another device about the size of his laptop, just a bit thicker, and sat it on the table. "This, gentleman, can pick up and intercept the cell phones in the area and act as a cell tower without the user knowing anything is different with their connection. It's called a Stingray."

Nate stared at him as he shook his head. "So, it could detect the phone number of the pick-up guy for the organs?"

With a wink, Kai laughed. "Let's hope it gives us precise location information in time to stop the next murder, guys. I also got to chat with the charter captain. He doesn't seem to be a threat. But as I left, his door was open where the knives are on the wall when he fillets. I pride myself on not letting anyone sneak up behind me, but he did. Scared the shit out of me, I won't lie. I don't normally set myself up like that. It *was* a little creepy."

Kai checked as the phone program pulled the information they needed and the numbers that were called. "And there it is! We have our information. I just need a printer. I'll make sure both of you have a copy of this once it's printed."

Rafe led Kai with his laptop to the private office, and Rafe connected the printer cord to Kai's laptop. The reports were printed off, and Rafe made two other copies for each of them, giving the original to Kai. "Now, let's go match up the numbers."

Back in the conference room, Kai gave the last four digits of one of the numbers, and Rafe scoured the cell tower printout. He watched Rafe highlight a few matching numbers, and Kai gave him another number, again highlighting where it was located.

Rafe shook his head and glanced up at Kai. "These have to be burner phones, and all calls are made and received after eleven pm or later."

Kai saw several numbers highlighted. "Now, also highlight the latitude and longitude of each tower and we'll mark them on the map you've got up there on the war board."

As Kai called out the locations, he watched Rafe mark one near Hag Stone, one at each tower in Pebble Cove, and one up near Ravensville. "These tower marks are near where the bodies were found except for the tower in Ravensville. You said no body has been found there. Perhaps our killer lives there...or the buyer. And note the times of each call. The most recent was made near Ravensville. That just causes questions! The calls seem to be made about three weeks apart and the latest three days ago!"

Nate set his cup down and looked at Rafe. "We've not done any searching in the Ravensville area. I think we should schedule an investigation there. Hey, will the Stingray pick up call locations if we keep it connected for the next week?"

"Yes, but the call patterns show only one or two calls together, and the Ravensville calls have already had two. I doubt they'll be stupid enough to make a random call, but I'd be happy to leave the Stingray here and running. Or, I can monitor it at the cabin. I have alarms I can set up to monitor certain times, like eleven pm to two am."

"Keep it with you then. You've got both of our numbers should an alarm sound, so please call one or both of us." Rafe capped his highlighter and sat back down. "These are the locations we were aware of. Thank you for bringing us this information."

"I just feel there's something on the horizon, in the planning stages, so to speak," Nate commented as he picked up the coffee cups and creamer.

"I'll give my contact a call who works at the lab. Maybe she can make it over here before you have to leave." Rafe gathered the papers and highlighters.

Kai packed up the machines. "I'll head back to the cabin and get this set up. You know where to find me." He glanced at both men. "Text me first. I want to head toward Ravensville over the next few days and shift to see what I find. I'll let you know." Kai headed to his bike, carefully packed the laptop and Stingray in his saddlebag, and rode toward the cabins. Today had been a good day information-wise. He didn't think the charter captain was a threat after talking with him last night.

On his way through town, Kai saw a butcher shop...*Deadly Cuts*. The name matched the creepiness of a few other places in town. A good rib steak sounded tempting, and he drove his bike into a spot in front of the store. He took his helmet off, hung it on the handlebars, and glanced to his right on the way in. His heart stopped instantly when he saw a woman who resembled Kinsley talking with someone a block away. He blinked to make sure he was seeing correctly. The slender woman's ponytail hung down her back and her gestures had to belong to Kinsley.

Shit.

Before she saw him, he quickly stepped into the shop as the bell on the door jingled. Kai gathered his thoughts but seeing her here in Pebble Cove made his head swim. Along with the odor of fresh meat.

"Can I help you?"

The man behind the meat counter wore an apron and dark-framed glasses, with a bald head. His white oxford shirt was pressed and the collar opened at the top. Pristine came to mind, but blood was smeared on his apron, obviously from cutting the meat. Out of the ordinary if he were OCD. Beyond his butcher table, a long wide magnet hung on the wall that held his choice of knives, and Kai made a mental note that it was the second such knife holder he'd seen here. The man used his little finger to press his glasses higher up on his nose.

"Two rib steaks, please." Kai positioned himself so his back wasn't toward the door. The place was immaculate but, then again, it had to be for a butcher shop.

"Would you like to pick them out?"

Kai met the man's steady gaze. "I'm sure you're a good judge of cuts. I trust you. That'll be it for today."

The butcher picked out and wrapped the steaks. "You new in town? I know most everyone."

"I am. I'm here for a week or two. Not sure yet. Do you live in town? It looks like a great place to raise kids." Kai wondered how much information the man would give him.

He took Kai's money. "No, I don't live in town. Thank you for stopping in. Enjoy your stay."

The man watched Kai leave and was still watching him when Kai snapped on his helmet. He glanced down the street in time to see Kinsley walk in the other direction. The sway of her hips would always make his heart skip. He cursed himself for screwing up years ago, whatever it was that had pissed her off so much.

One day he'd ask her.

When he rode away, he turned a block before her so she wouldn't see him, and he headed for the cabins just outside of town. Knowing she was here would screw with his head. He should have known she'd be close since Rafe was here, and Rafe had never brought up her name. How close were those two?

* * * * *

Nate washed out the coffee mugs, dried them, and put them back by the coffee pot. "I like Kai. He seems to know his stuff. I think we made some headway today. I'm curious to talk with Morgan tonight to see if she has any weird feelings about these murders like we do. She's pretty good at sensing when something is off."

"He does seem pretty sharp. I wouldn't mind shifting with him and seeing where he investigates. Maybe I'll mention it tomorrow."

"I'm heading out to do rounds, then I'm stopping at *Magic Knots Bakery* to get more of those strawberries that Margo gave us. Morgan loved them."

"How's she doing with the move?"

"She's still unpacking in between being at the store and home. It doesn't give her much time. Call me if you hear anything from Kai." Nate climbed into his rig to do his rounds, excited that they could be on the brink of finding their killer. The public was getting jittery.

The hair on the back of Nate's neck stood up, and his jaw clenched as he drove through town. His gaze scanned the sidewalks for anything strange. He flexed his fingers on the steering wheel, his claws itching to come out, as his wolf sensed danger nearby. Villagers shopped or talked in groups outside the stores. Everything appeared normal.

He heard the crash before he saw it.

Up ahead, a car had t-boned another, and one of the cars was familiar.

Morgan's car had been hit broadside and spun around in front of him.

A man stood on the corner watching, and Nate recognized him immediately as he sped his truck up and parked at the corner.

As he jumped out, the man vanished before his eyes.

He blinked, knowing damn well he knew who it was that disappeared. Nate looked for the man in all directions before he ran to Morgan's car, relieved that she didn't appear hurt. He tore open her door, nearly ripping it from the hinges, thankful the accident hadn't been worse. "Are you alright, babe?"

"I am, but I know I looked before I pulled out from the side street. I don't understand." She stepped out and into Nate's arms. His fingers threaded through her hair as he hugged her tight, attempting to calm his racing heart, then held her out and met her gaze.

"I saw him, on the corner right here, at the same time you were hit. I know it was *him,* and he vanished before I got out of my truck. Let me check on the other driver." He squeezed her upper arms. "I'll be right back."

Nate ran over to check the other driver and gave Rafe a call to meet him at the scene. The other passenger had a bump on his head but no blood. "Officer, I didn't even see her until I hit her car!"

"It's fine. As long as you aren't hurt. She said she didn't see your car either. Let's get the wrecker here, and exchange insurance information. Do you have a ride home?"

"I can call my wife. I'm not hurt, just a bit baffled how this happened."

Nate went back to Morgan, his heart still racing and his mind trying to block out the car accident years ago that fatally claimed his first wife. He didn't have time for his mind to react to that memory.

Morgan was fine; it would all be fine.

She took his face in her hands to get his attention. "I know your past just flashed through your mind about your wife. Are you alright? I'm fine, babe. Who was the man you saw that vanished? That isn't possible unless..."

He pulled her hands from his face at the same time she realized *who* had vanished.

"Are you saying Danteleon caused this accident?" She looked around the area, her gaze scanning for the stranger.

"Morgan, I know what I saw, and I saw him vanish before my eyes. It was *him*. He was here, dammit! I knew it was too much to hope that he'd leave us alone!"

Rafe pulled his sheriff car next to Morgan's. "What happened? Everyone is alright?"

Nate stepped over to talk with Rafe. "At the same time I saw the accident, I saw Danteleon standing on the corner watching the whole thing. I'm sure he caused it. Before I could get out of my rig, he vanished into thin air!"

"*Son-of-a-bitch!* Her father needs to find a way to end all of this! I'll go talk with the other driver. See if you can find anything out. He needs to be stopped before someone dies!"

Once the wrecker had hauled off the vehicles, Nate got Morgan into his truck. He reached over for her hand and headed toward *Magic Knots Bakery* to surprise her. She squeezed his fingers when he pulled into a parking spot. "You're coming in with me. I'm not about to leave you out here alone for *him* to find. Let's go get more strawberries."

Nate held the door open, and they went in. A squeal from the back kitchen greeted them when they admired the delicacies behind the glass.

"It's so good to see you two. I knew you'd be in for more of those chocolate strawberries! I'm glad you liked them. How about a deal? A free one for every two you buy!"

Morgan laughed. "Oh, Margo! You're such a sweetheart. They were delicious. Nate enjoyed a bite or two."

"She doesn't share well when it comes to treats like those."

"Well...I doubt she shares you either, Nate. My loss. Now, how many should we box up?"

"Let's do six." He glanced down at Morgan, and her eyes lit up. "You can pay me later." His wink made her smile as her cheeks filled with color.

Margo wrapped them in tissue and tied a bow on the box, then put them in a cute little bag. "You two love birds enjoy those. Thank you for coming in!"

Morgan took the bag and thanked her. Nate scanned the area outside the bakery to be sure the dark warlock wasn't anywhere near them. He got Morgan seated with her chocolate delights and got in himself. He held her hand on the way home, glad that the accident had not been worse. It was late afternoon with a blue sky, yet he still had to finish his rounds. He hated to just drop her off at the house alone, but the wards were up so she would be safe.

Her grip tightened on his hand. "I know you have to finish your day. I'll be fine. I have lots to unpack yet. I'm working on my herb room, and Angela is bringing over the dried herbs for me from her garden. I've got my jars and bottles ready. Don't worry about me. I'll see you when you get back, hon." She leaned over to kiss him before she got out.

His heart tugged at how close he came to the accident being worse than it was, and he couldn't let worry run his life. Their time together would be wonderful, and he'd take each day as it came. Nate watched her go in and he returned to town in search of Danteleon.

* * * * *

Morgan set the pretty bag of desserts in the refrigerator and set her purse on the side table. As she looked around at her new home, she still couldn't believe the change in her life over the past few months. She and Nate couldn't be happier, and their future would be exciting...if her father could get rid of Danteleon!

After she grabbed her phone from her purse, she went down the hall to her new herb room in the same end of the house near their bedroom. The room Nate gave her was huge, which gave her plenty of space for shelves.

Morgan tipped her head, envisioned a wall full of shelving, and with a swirl of her hand, the shelves lined the entire far wall. She laughed at herself and how easy it was to make things happen. The boxes of various sized jars sat on the floor. She waved her hand, and the jars drifted out of the boxes and onto the shelves. When she snapped her fingers, the boxes disappeared. Now, she needed a work space and a desk. Walking toward the window on the other wall, she placed a high work table for her herbs, and a mortar and pestle to grind thorns, like Angela had used around their property.

A nice desk with filing drawers would be great to work at, with space to use her scrying mirror. Morgan pointed to the wall on the other side of the window and a large desk appeared with plenty of space to store everything. *Where had she packed her beautiful new mirror that she bought at Suzy's antique shop?*

She set her phone on the desk and started rummaging through the boxes from her apartment. Morgan brought two of her smaller lamps; one would be perfect for the desk; the other one would set on the work table. When she found the mirror, she ripped off the tissue paper and admired the black glass with the ornate frame. It had a stand attached to the back and she set it on the desk, then sat down in the chair.

Satisfied with herself, she looked around. The desk lamp came on as dusk approached outside and lit the room. Once she and Angela filled her jars with herbs, blessed salts, and various thorns for future spells, she would be able to begin her learning. Her gaze went to the mirror as she admired her reflection in the black glass...when a blue mist suddenly began to swirl inside the mirror.

She gasped at first, since she'd never scryed with it yet. The image appeared blurred as forms began to take shape, of a dark forest and a deep ravine. It was as if she were there. Upon closer viewing, the huge ravine came into clear view and a body lay at the bottom, covered in leaves. Morgan touched her throat and sat back in her chair, unable to take her eyes from the glass. Just as quickly, the mist took away the images and returned to a black mirror. Surely she should tell Nate what she'd seen in the vision.

"Oh, my goddess!" Morgan leaned closer to the mirror, but nothing more showed itself. Dusk had created eerie shadows in every corner around the room, and she could have sworn that her peripheral vision played tricks on her.

A disturbance in the air of the room occurred and Izzy stood in front of Morgan's new shelves admiring her handy work. "You *are* getting good at this! I like what you've done to the room!"

Izzy ran her hand over the work table and stood there a moment. "I remember spending hours at my own table, concocting my salts and crushing thorns to ward off the evil. You'll do well here, my dear."

Morgan could only smile, wishing she could hug the apparition of the old woman. "I'm so glad you approve, Izzy. I've missed you. Thank you for coming today."

The woman rolled her eyes. "Regarding the vision you just witnessed, I figured you'd need someone at your side."

"You don't miss a thing, do you? I'm glad you popped in when you did. I wish I knew the exact location of the body so I could be of more help to Nate."

"Jadis will help you hone your skills. You'll do just fine in the future. I'm glad you're happy here. I still visit my old apartment now and then. You didn't bring your grimoire."

"Logan and Mandy are going to read it tonight so that he's ready to train with Jadis tomorrow afternoon."

Izzy nodded as she peered out the window. "The view of the ocean beyond the pool is nice. Be sure to keep the wards renewed. Don't give *him* a way in here." Izzy placed a bag tied with a purple ribbon on Morgan's work table. "I brought you Dragon's Blood to protect your home and property. A pinch under the mattress will help ensure future babies!" She winked and smiled. "I also brought you Bloodwort to help open your psychic abilities."

"Izzy, thank you, but I don't plan on any more babies! Especially not at my age!"

The old woman placed her fingers beneath Morgan's chin, then turned her face from side to side. "You are but a child compared to my age, my dear. Never say never! Do remember that I'm only a thought away should you need me. I'll see you later."

In an instant, Izzy was gone but the scent of her perfume lingered, and Morgan hated to see her leave. The woman always gave her new information, and today she left her more herbs and powders for her jars. She picked up the bag and sniffed it, only to curl her lip at the smell. Perhaps, one would help her mind make sense of the visions in the mirror.

When her phone buzzed, Morgan jumped, sending her heart into her throat. She had to quit being so jumpy! Angela's photo appeared. She answered it, still a bit shaken. "Hi Angela!"

"Hey, is now a good time to *pop* over with stuff for your herb room?"

Her excitement took over, sending her worry to the back of her mind. "It is! I just got the jars unpacked and organized. I can't wait. I'll meet you in our kitchen."

Chapter 5

Morgan hurried to the kitchen, opened a white wine, and got two glasses down. A flutter of air announced Angela's arrival, her arms filled the bags and baskets overflowing with herbs of every kind. "Here, let me take some of those." Morgan set the baskets on the kitchen island. "I've just opened a Riesling for us. After my car accident this afternoon, I need something. Nate said he saw Danteleon standing on the corner when my accident happened."

Angela gasped. "I hope you weren't hurt."

"I'm sure I'll feel it in the morning. Let's take these into my office and drink our wine while we organize."

"I can't wait to see it." Angela followed Morgan, her arms still filled with boxes and bags.

"Oh, goddess, this is so big! What a nice place to work! Nate's home is huge, and you are one lucky woman!" Angela set the bags on the floor and admired the shelves.

Morgan set the wine and glasses on the work table, and the baskets on the floor nearby. "I don't know how to thank you enough for drying all of these."

"This will be fun. I brought you an herb book that tells you what different herbs and salts do and how to use them. Your grimoire should have different spells and how to use the herbs and crushed thorns for good spells to ward off evil. At least you have room for the books you'll want to have on hand, too."

Not allowing herself to get overwhelmed, Morgan gathered a few jars and put them on the work table. She told Angela about the bag of herbs Izzy had left her.

Angela began pulling sage, rosemary, thyme, and basil from the baskets and arranged them on the table. From another box, she took out salts in different colors, each one having its own power to help ward off spirits, purify blessings, or bring love to those who need it. After a few hours, they'd completed the tasks and admired the shelves as Morgan poured the last of the wine in their glasses.

Nate appeared in the doorway with a huge smile on his face. "I'm glad you made this room your own. I see you two have been busy. I like this."

Seeing Nate made Morgan take in a breath. She still couldn't believe that a woman before her hadn't caught his attention, and she was now the recipient of his affection. He stepped into the room, and she put her arm around his waist, her fingers roaming over the muscles of his ribs. "Angela has been kind enough to dry all of these for me and show me what I need to know."

Nate looked at Angela. "Thank you. I'm sure it will all come in handy and keep her out of trouble."

Angela laughed. "I don't know about that, but she *is* a fast learner. I've no doubt she'll be spinning spells in no time."

"I need a beer so I can join the party."

Morgan followed him to the kitchen, and Angela set her glass near the sink. "I'll be getting out of your way. Enjoy your office, and please call me should you need anything. I might have a few other items down at the store. You should stop in sometime."

After she thanked Angela, the woman teleported back to her home with Kinsley, and Morgan got a glass of ice water. She had to tell Nate what she'd seen in the mirror, but would he believe her? The afternoon had been filled with many events she needed to think over.

Nate pulled out a bar stool and sat at the island. "I'm really glad you got your office organized. It looks great. And the shelving?" He raised a sexy brow at her.

She giggled. "It was just a swirl of my hand and all of it went where I wanted. I couldn't resist. And my scrying mirror has a nice place on my desk."

"Does it speak to you?"

"I haven't really had a chance to learn how to use it, but...an image *did* show itself before Angela arrived."

Nate tipped his head and drew his brows together. "...and?"

Morgan chewed her lower lip, not sure how to explain what she'd seen. "There is no easy way to say this, but it showed me dark woods and a very deep ravine. Nate...there was a body at the bottom covered with leaves. I only saw the vision for a moment, but I have no idea where the location is."

"I was going to ask if you've had any idea of what we might find in the future. I guess that answers my question. Not that we need another murder." He reached over and covered her hand with his, and she gripped his warm fingers. "I'll tell Rafe, and we'll figure out where to look. Did you see any other signs that might indicate where?"

"I didn't. I'm sorry. Maybe I can scry again later and something might show up. It did shake me up a little, since it's the first vision I've seen in my mirror. I wasn't sure it would actually work." She met his gaze and knew he believed in her abilities. "I love you. The fact that you have faith in what I am, and are still hanging around, makes my heart happy."

Nate squeezed her hand. "You can't scare me off. I'm not going anywhere, but I am determined to see this dark warlock gone and out of our lives. He tried to kill you today!"

She chewed at her lip. "I know. I need to contact my dad to see what he's heard. Oh, by the way, Logan and Jadis will be training in the backyard tomorrow, and I'm going to join them. The wards are up, so we should be fully protected from outside forces."

"You've had an eventful day. Let's go relax and watch TV for a bit. Then we can sample those berries we bought!" He winked at her, and she joined him in their double, loveseat recliners.

* * * * *

Still at the station, Rafe finished his notes on the accident but left out anything that had to do with the person who disappeared. It had been another exhausting day. As he closed his notes and filed them, his phone vibrated.

Destiny's name showed up, and he held his breath for a moment before answering her call. "Hey, what's new? How's the world of tissue matching?"

Thoughts ran together in his head regarding her possible visit and how to fit that in and see Kinsley, too. Their relationship suddenly barged into his mind knowing he would be hurting her in the end. *What a mess!* Rafe massaged the tense muscle in his neck.

Her laughter drifted through the phone to make him smile. "Well, I have a few days to spend in Pebble Cove if we can work that out. Is tomorrow too soon? I know you had lots of questions for me."

"The sooner you get here, the better. I have a few people I want you to meet, and Kinsley will be thrilled to see you. Make a reservation at the cabins and be sure to tell Kins when you'll be in town."

"It's a deal! See you tomorrow, sunshine!"

Rafe put down his phone and scrubbed his face with his hands. How this would play out was anyone's guess. His relationship with Kinsley was important to him, but for years, she'd held back for some crazy reasoning about her heartbreak years ago. Now, fearing another broken heart, she refused to commit to moving in with him or taking their feelings for each other any further.

Having Destiny here, and the way she affected his emotions, would certainly be hard to hide in front of Kinsley. *Damn it!* Fate was again rearing its ugly head. His love life certainly wasn't anything to brag about. Now he had two women that his heart wanted.

Just face the music and play it out.

He grabbed his keys, shut off the lights, and headed home to an empty house.

When he pulled into his driveway, the lights in the kitchen were on, but there wasn't another rig in the driveway. Rafe kept his hand on his sidearm as he approached the porch. On the front door, a sticky note alerted him to come in the door slowly and wait.

Kinsley signed it.

She always seemed to come through for him when he needed her. As he opened the door, he smelled baked potatoes and rib steak. Rafe couldn't keep the smile from his face, and he waited like she'd instructed.

"Hey sexy!" She stood at the kitchen island wearing black leggings with a deep V-neck, white silky top, her long dark hair over one shoulder, and her eyes sparkling like cut emeralds. Her lips were like those of a goddess. He stepped toward her and held out his arms. When she stepped into them and hugged him, her vanilla scent filled his senses as her warm lips touched his neck, sending electrical shocks through his system. God, he needed this every day! Her tongue trailed up toward his ear. "You make me crazy, shifter."

Rafe closed his eyes and let the moment sink into his memory. They needed more times like these. To hold her close made him feel whole and loved which he wasn't sure he should get used to, but tonight she was here and he'd love her back.

"You can't even come close to what you make *me* feel when you're with me." He cupped her face and took her mouth with his, their tongues caressing each other, making his world lop-sided. Tasting the whiskey she'd sipped earlier sent his thoughts into the bedroom, but dinner would have to come first. "You taste so good, babe." He touched his forehead to hers. "Thank you for this. I needed it today."

Her hand smoothed down his cheek. "Let's have a drink and enjoy dinner. Tell me how your day was."

The table had been set, and Kinsley filled his glass with ice. She grabbed the whiskey from the freezer and poured them both a drink. "For starters, Morgan was in an accident downtown today. Nate said he saw Danteleon on the corner at the same time he heard the crash, and the man disappeared right in front of him."

Kinsley gasped. "So, he caused the accident? I hate that he might be creating more trouble." With a wave of her hand, the steak and potatoes drifted over to the table.

Rafe smiled at her antics. "According to Nate. The other gentleman wasn't hurt either, and their cars are already at the repair shop. Nate took Morgan to get more of the chocolate strawberries at the *Magic Knot* and took her home."

"I think Angela was taking the herbs over today for her jars. I'm sure they had fun. I hope that was the worst part of your day."

"It was. The best part was coming home tonight." He watched her over the rim of his glass, his mind creating a scene for later of her naked and waiting.

"I wanted to do something special for you. I know you've been working hard on the murders. I hope that investigator had some good news for you, or at least, some ideas on how to stop what's happening."

"He did have ideas for us that will allow us to track a few things. I'm not sure if we need to do some searching up by Ravensville, but indications are leading that way. I also heard from Destiny this afternoon."

"Does she have any word for you on the tissue matching that might lead to anything?"

"I'm not sure. She *did* say she was coming into town tomorrow and is staying at one of the cabins because she loved staying there last time. I told her to make sure she let you know."

"I haven't checked my phone, but it'll be great to see her again."

Rafe finished his drink and got up to refill it. "I want her to talk with this new investigator. He might have a few questions for her that I've not thought to ask. We'll know more when she arrives." Before he sat back down, he stood behind Kinsley, moved her silky hair away from her neck, and kissed her there. The scent of vanilla surrounded her. "You smell too good for a man as hungry as I am."

As he sat back down, Kinsley reached for his hand, and he took hers. Their eyes searched each other, and feelings swam in her heart. "I hope I can satisfy all of your cravings tonight." She gave him a sexy wink and sipped her drink. "Let's eat our steak before it gets cold."

Rafe couldn't deny his hunger. He hadn't eaten all day, and the steak was medium rare, just how he liked it. Kinsley chatted about her day, and he tried to listen, but his thoughts were on their after-dinner escapades. Dealing with his feelings regarding their relationship would smooth out on their own. He had no idea how things would go once Destiny got into town, but he *did* remember what being near her did to him.

Tonight, his dreams would come true with Kinsley. That's all that mattered right now.

* * * * *

Kinsley awoke with Rafe's arm over her hip, snuggled up behind her, and her phone vibrating on the nightstand. When she reached for it, Rafe caressed down her hip and over her thigh.

The call was from Destiny! "Hello!"

"Hey! Did I wake you? I know it's early, but I'm almost to Pebble Cove. I texted you last night but never heard back from you."

She sat up in bed and pulled the sheet up as Rafe lifted his arm to settle it over her thighs. "Rafe mentioned you were coming. Let me know once you get checked in, and I'll pop over. I can't wait to see you!"

"Sure thing. I should be there in about an hour. See you later, chicky!"

Kinsley put her phone back on the stand and snuggled back down beside Rafe. He put his arm around her as she put her arm over his waist. He still smelled so good that her body reacted on its own. Again, her senses nagged at her about not committing to their relationship. *After the night they'd had, how could she even think he'd break her heart?* Waking up in his arms felt so special, and she placed a kiss on his chest.

A finger beneath her chin lifted her face up to his. Their eyes met, and her center tightened. His blue eyes made her heart flip every time he looked at her with that much desire. "This is really nice, having you in my bed in the morning, but I can feel your thoughts reeling around inside that pretty head of yours."

"It feels right being here. You take such good care of me. I need to do better on my part."

He kissed her nose. "There's no pressure. I'm thankful you showed up to surprise me last night. Dinner was delicious."

"Destiny just called. She'll be in town in an hour and will call once she's checked in. I know you wanted to talk with her today. I hope she can help out somehow."

"I guess we better hit the shower then, eh?" He kissed her nose one more time, and she rolled out the other side, showing him her lovely naked ass. She knew her gym workouts certainly paid off for *his* view.

* * * * *

An hour later, Kinsley rode her Harley over to the cabins, happy that Destiny had decided to visit Pebble Cove again. She needed to do better by staying in touch with her best friend before she lost her.

Coming up on the cabin's driveway, she slowed and rode down to where the customers parked. Destiny's vehicle was at the second cabin, and a Harley was parked at the first one. Kinsley pulled in between the two. As she got off and removed her helmet, a strong sense of danger tugged at her. Nothing nearby seemed to be out of order, and she heard Destiny open the door on the front porch.

Destiny hugged her and hung on to Kinsley for a second longer, then stepped away. "I've missed you. We need to stay in touch more! Come on. I thought you might need a mimosa!"

"You know what I like!" Kinsley hung her leather jacket on a chair and had to peek out the back door to admire the view of the beach. She never tired of living here on the Pacific Coast.

"Speaking of what you like...wait till you see the hunk staying next door. Hot damn, he's built!"

Kinsley turned to accept the tall mimosa. "Maybe you need to take over a cup of sugar. Tell him you came over to sweeten his day."

"Sounds like a plan. I could do that." Destiny led the way onto the back porch so they could watch the ocean waves wash over the sand.

Kinsley got comfy in the Adirondack chair. The orange mimosa tasted like heaven. "Rafe said he'd be by shortly to talk with you. I hope someone has ideas on stopping these murders."

Destiny set her glass on the wooden table that sat between their chairs. "I'm not sure what kind of help I can be, but I'll give him any information I can."

A man walked out on the beach and Kinsley immediately took in a breath. Why would she feel such animosity when she had no idea who he was. He flipped his blonde hair to the side and turned his muscular frame toward her.

"Oh my god, Kins, that's the guy next door! You've got to meet him if he comes up here. His blue eyes will strip you naked and eat you up from a distance, I swear!"

A woman played in the sand with her two children when suddenly her daughter darted into the water, splashing as she ran, without her mother's knowledge. The muscular man rushed toward the child and scooped her up just as she went under. He calmed her as he carried her back, in his strong arms, to her shocked parent, who hugged her daughter. She thanked him, he tousled the hair of her brother and then turned toward the cabins.

As the man got closer, Kinsley dropped her glass, and it spilled over the porch. She bent down to pick up the unbroken glass.

"Hey, no worries. I'll get you a new refill, but yep, that's the effect he had on me, too." Destiny took her own glass in to freshen it up.

When she returned with the drinks, the stranger was half-way to them. Kinsley's lungs felt like a tight band had wrapped around her ribs, prohibiting her from breathing. "Oh, my goddess, Destiny!"

She looked at Destiny as she spread out her fingers.

"Isn't he gorgeous?" Destiny set their glasses on the table, then gasped when she looked at Kinsley. "You're as white as a sheet. Are you alright?" Destiny grabbed her arm and shook her. "Kins, you need to breathe."

"Hi ladies!" The man removed his aviator sunglasses and flashed them a huge smile. His wet shirt molded to his chest and drew Kinsley's attention.

She slowly moved her gaze up to meet the blue eyes that had haunted her dreams for years, which sparked the memories that flooded her brain. *An Adonis from her past who had disappeared without a word!* They were the same eyes she'd seen in the mirror at the Dragon's Lair and an angry fire lit up inside of her. "What the hell are you doing here?"

Destiny put a hand on Kinsley's shoulder. "Hon, stay calm, he's renting the cabin next door. Do you two know each other?"

Without taking her eyes from the stranger, Kinsley answered her. "Destiny, meet Kai McGarrett. We haven't seen each other since high school." Her jaw tightened as her anger boiled over, remembering that he'd never contacted her after she went off to college.

"Oh my, gosh, Kins. This is...."

"Exactly." She stared into his gaze that never wavered.

Kai stepped close enough to put one foot up onto the porch. "Kins, I think we saw each other a week ago...at that bar. You're still beautiful. Even more so when you're in shock."

"Wait, I'm confused." Destiny still held onto her arm and made Kinsley look at her. "This is the crush you had from high school and refused to see any other guy through college because of *him?*" Destiny stared at Kai. "I don't understand. Why is it that you never called her?"

"I'd like to know why, too?" Kinsley stared at the man, barely able to think a straight thought. Her lip curled at the side before she picked up her drink and downed it all in one gulp.

Without losing eye contact with Kinsley, Kai answered Destiny. "I'm not sure what happened after she left for college. I guess I assumed she wanted her own life, so I didn't bother her, and went about *my* own life. I joined the military and that's taken up my time since then."

Kinsley swallowed hard as she listened to his explanation, not sure whether to believe him or not.

"Then you have no idea about the broken heart you left behind, do you? I've heard so much about you that I feel like I know you. But you certainly hold up to what I've heard, let me tell *you*."

Chapter 6

Kai's gaze was still glued to Kinsley, his eyebrows covered by his longer hair that swept over his forehead. Her mind couldn't even put together a sentence because his presence made her too rattled. *Why didn't I ever try to call him? What a waste of twenty-five years!* Her heart ached with him standing in front of her. No words even came to mind as she dealt with the loss of so much time.

"McGarrett! Get the fuck away from them! Now!"

Shock at the loud, angry words hit Kinsley like ice water as Rafe stormed around the corner of the first cabin. Rafe's shirt began to rip as his shoulders expanded, along with his uniform pants when his thighs grew stronger. When he leapt at Kai, the man backed away as claws appeared from the fingertips of both men. Kai's shoulders enlarged bigger than a weight lifter, like something she'd never seen on a man.

Right before her eyes, both men shifted into half-human and half-animal, and pounced on one another. Teeth visible as shreds of clothing tossed in the air. The wolf went air-bound first as the cougar attacked. They rolled, dead set on killing one another. The cougar swiped its claw to catch the front shoulder of the wolf, only enraging it more.

The wolf fought against the huge cougar as Kinsley watched, and she screamed as Destiny held her back. "You'll be ripped apart if you run out there. Oh my gosh, Kins! What the hell is going on?"

The animals rolled over each other and made their struggle toward the water. Before they got to the waves, the cougar pinned the wolf, his teeth inches from the wolf's neck. Kinsley knew it was Rafe that was in trouble. She had no idea Kai could shift into a cougar. Her feelings swarmed in her head. Too much came at her at once. *How can I help either of them?* They need to figure this out on their own.

Kinsley couldn't bear the thought of either of them dying and knew she had to interfere. Pulling her arm back, as though she were throwing a softball, she tossed a golden red ball of fire through the air, aimed to knock the animals apart and stop the fight.

When the fireball hit the cougar, it leapt off the wolf, shook itself, and walked toward the sand, shaking his paws until he shifted back to human. He grabbed a towel nearby, laying on the beach, and wrapped his hips, but blood dripped from his arms. Kai glanced at Kinsley and could only stare at her.

The wolf rolled over and shifted back, shaking his head while he was on his hands and knees. When Rafe stood, he looked over his shoulder at Kinsley, then back to Kai.

"Quick, Destiny, go grab a bath towel." Glancing at Kinsley as though she had two heads, Destiny ran into the cabin for the towel. When she returned, Kinsley grabbed the towel and jumped off the porch. "Stay here, I'll be right back."

When she approached Rafe with the towel, she saw his chest covered in bloody claw marks. "Are you two *boys* about finished? For goddess' sake, can we stop this childish competition?"

Kinsley looked from Rafe to Kai, and back again. "What the hell?" She waited for an answer.

Rafe took the towel and wrapped it around his hips. "I don't know what came over me, Kins. I truly don't."

Kai examined the bleeding cuts on his arms. "I know mate-violence when I see it!" He glared at Rafe as he tossed his hair away from his eyes. "You can't be mated to both of them, asshole, so which one is it...Kinsley...or *Destiny*?"

As realization sank into Kinsley's brain that Rafe may be protecting Destiny, her anger exploded and began to burn a huge circle in the grass around them as she stared at Rafe, waiting for his answer. Fire raged from her fingertips, and she spread them out at her sides. "I'm waiting for an answer!"

"Kinsley! What the hell?" Destiny called out from the porch at the same time Kinsley saw a figure emerging from the water and walking toward the shore.

The creature walked on two legs, and he twisted his head as he cracked his neck. With teeth showing, it howled at the sky and once it reached the sand, ran full speed toward Kinsley.

Both men immediately shifted back to race toward the creature, knocking it backward onto the sand when the cougar's teeth sank into the creature's throat.

She watched in horror and waited for the death shake.

Kinsley knew the creature could only be one thing...Danteleon!

She tossed another fireball as Rafe grabbed the creature's leg to drag him toward Kinsley. The fireball exploded when it hit the creature, spreading fire over the animal. The cougar leapt out of the way in time for the burning creature to race back into the water and disappear.

She didn't expect the wolf or cougar to follow the creature, but they both dove under water. Kinsley shook out her hands to stop the fire, then waved her hand to douse the flames on the grass and return it back to normal.

Destiny was at her side when the men re-emerged from the water without the creature. "I can't believe what I just witnessed. Maybe I'm dreaming and I'll wake up soon. This is definitely a nightmare!"

How could I even begin to explain any of this to my best friend? Destiny had no powers that Kinsley knew of. She was totally a mortal. *Where do I even start?* Closing her eyes, Kinsley searched for an answer. A mere mortal couldn't even begin to understand their world.

Destiny took Kinsley's hands and turned them over as she examined them. "This isn't a nightmare is it? I saw something from a horror movie."

She met her best friend's gaze, her beautiful blue eyes pooling with tears. "There's a lot to explain, hon. I'm not even sure where to start."

The men walked toward the beach and before they got to the sand, Kinsley turned with Destiny to go back up to the cabin. Silence filled the short walk to the porch. "Let's go inside. We both need some of that champagne."

Destiny sat at the lodgepole table in the kitchen, and Kinsley poured her a glass of champagne, then filled her own glass. She sat with Destiny and downed the bubbly liquid. Knowing they'd all need a stronger drink, Kinsley snapped her fingers to produce the bottle of whiskey and four tumblers.

"Holy shit, Kins! When...."

She held up her hand to stop her friend. "I need a minute, Des." Kinsley broke the seal and filled the four tumblers halfway with the golden liquid. She drank hers and refilled it, then pushed one over to Destiny. "Drink up. You're going to need that."

Without question, Destiny downed hers and held out her glass for more. Kinsley refilled it.

"So...you're a witch with abilities? That isn't even possible. And what the hell happened with the guys? Fuck, Kinsley!" Destiny downed the whiskey in her glass and wanted more.

Kinsley didn't pour her more just yet. With such a shock, Destiny wouldn't feel the effects of the whiskey until it was too late if Kinsley wasn't careful. She laid her fingers over Destiny's forearm. "I had to keep it a secret, Des. Today was not an ordinary day."

"No shit!" Destiny picked up Kinsley's hand and examined her fingertips again. "These were on fire!" Destiny rubbed between her eyebrows, then took the hair scrunchy from her wrist, gathered her smooth red hair, and pulled it all into a ponytail.

With her hands wrapped around her glass, Kinsley rolled it between her fingers, searching for the right words. "Both of my parents are witches and so are my brother and sister. We didn't realize we had abilities until after we were forty. That happens with many witches and warlocks. Anyone you'll ever meet could be a witch or warlock and you would never know. We don't do magick in front of mortals ...usually. Today was an exception, and you saw a demon come out of the water!"

Kinsley thought back to what may have triggered Rafe to start a fight with Kai. He'd mentioned something about mate violence, but she didn't understand that. Then she glanced up at Destiny.

Does Rafe have feelings for her?

Ripples of shock started in her chest and slowly spread throughout her body. *How long had he known?* That's what the anger was from! The memory of last night in Rafe's arms flashed blood-red in her mind. He'd known *then* that Destiny was coming into town yet still spent last night with her. *But I've led him on for three years without committing!* Kinsley downed her whiskey, clenched her jaw, and waited for the burn from her throat to her stomach.

When the screen door opened and the guys stepped in, both she and Destiny turned to see the blood still seeping from their wounds. Kinsley snapped her fingers and bandages, alcohol, cotton balls, and tape appeared on the table.

Kinsley stood. "Here, both of you, sit. Now!"

They tucked their towels at the waist and without a word, sat where they were instructed. Kinsley handed cotton and alcohol to Destiny so she could clean up Rafe's wounds.

As Kinsley stood at Kai's side, she wet the cotton ball to dab at the cuts on his chest. "This is going to sting." The deep cut ran alongside of the cougar tattoo on his right chest. *How fitting.*

"It won't be the first time. I'm sure it won't be the last." Kai met her gaze, which was her undoing. The icy blueness of his eyes bombarded her with memories of their high school days, and she bit into her lower lip. Watching what she was doing would be better than looking into those eyes again.

Damn it!

What the hell had gone wrong with our relationship and how did we lose touch?

Kai grabbed her hand, and she tried to tug away. He took the cotton ball, and kissed the center of her palm, then made a circle with his tongue. He looked up at her. "I'm not sure why, but I can hear your thoughts. I'm sorry for whatever the reason was that made you so angry with me." He held out the cotton ball for her to finish. "Make it hurt more if that makes you feel better. I can take it."

She sucked in her lower lip, met his gaze and doused the cotton with extra alcohol. He jumped when she touched several new cuts.

"Shit. Alright, already!"

Kinsley peeked over at Rafe and Destiny when she heard Rafe wincing. "I'm as tough as he is. Just get it cleaned up, please. You're a doctor, so don't be squeamish."

"I'm tougher than you think, smart-ass!" Destiny went for the bottle of alcohol. "Hang on, tough guy!" She soaked the cotton ball and touched each of his cuts.

Rafe glanced at Kai. "We should have had a few whiskeys before you two started in on us."

Rafe reached for a tumbler and slid one over for Kai. The two drank it down in one gulp.

"I'm not a healer like my mother is. My brother got that ability, or none of this would be necessary." Kinsley wasn't sure she'd heal either of them even if she could. They both deserved the wounds they gave each other. She taped bandages on the cuts that didn't stop bleeding, and once they were both cleaned, Kinsley waved at the couch and clothing for both men appeared.

Kai shook his head and stared at Kinsley. "When did all this happen? After you turned twenty-one?"

She raised a brow at him. "Yes, but I could ask the same thing."

"I had already joined special forces when I found out I could shift at twenty-one. My parents never said a word. So, needless to say, once I went back home to see them, we had a few words."

Kinsley got rid of all the evidence of the wound clean-up. "You two change. I think we all have a lot to discuss."

Destiny shook out her hands before sitting down. She pushed her tumbler toward Kinsley. "We're going to need more than one bottle if we continue this discussion. I'm not sure I can handle all of this if I'm sober."

Kinsley snapped up a second bottle, emptied the first one into the tumblers, and sat at the table next to Destiny. The lodgepole table was square, not large by any means, but big enough for the small cabin. She reached out and covered Destiny's hand with hers. "We'll go slow so that you can understand all of what you witnessed today. You can't say a word to anyone. We can't have this getting out to the other mortals who live among us, but our abilities are real."

Destiny held her glass with both hands, her elbows on the table. "And that monster that came out of the ocean?"

The guys, dressed in clothing that Kinsley got for them, came out in time for them to hear her question. They each sat down and drank their whiskey before either of them said a word. Kai appeared as shocked as Destiny when the monster was mentioned.

Rafe refilled their glasses. "That monster happens to be a demon among the witch community. He was a warlock who went to the dark side and fought against others among the witch community. Now he's wanted by the Witch's Council, and they're hoping to somehow catch him so that he has to stand trial before them." He watched Destiny as her eyes widened with his story.

"He lives in the ocean?"

"No, but he's able to change his appearance to whatever he chooses to be, apparently. As soon as I saw the creature, I knew who it was. He was hoping to reach Kinsley."

"I'm confused. If he's on the dark side, what does she have to do with that?"

"He's actually after a close friend of hers, and if he nabs Kinsley, he ultimately gets to Morgan. There is magickal protection around all of the cabins to keep him out, but we were beyond the protection limits down at the beach."

"This is a lot to take in, but the whiskey is helping." She sipped her drink.

Rafe leaned his forearms on the table. "This isn't the way I wanted our day to go when you said you had time to visit Pebble Cove."

Kinsley set her glass down hard. "I'm a bit confused, too, and now that we're all here, I have a few questions of my own." Rafe cupped his tumbler and looked at the ceiling before she continued as she looked at Kai. "What do you have to do with all of this and why are you in town? I haven't seen, nor heard from you, in twenty-five years and suddenly here you are!"

"I'm a Special Agent investigator for a firm that works on difficult cases. A friend of Rafe's suggested he call me, and here I am." He moved his gaze between Kinsley and Rafe.

"He's already helped us pinpoint a few locations where cell phone activity showed up. Each of those points came together where three of the bodies were found. We now have a few more locations we need to check on which are out of the area and no bodies have been found up by Ravensville...yet."

After Kai set down his glass, he looked at Rafe, and joined in. "If the two of us shifted when we got to Ravensville, we could split up and search."

"I was hoping you'd suggest that. It's exactly what I want to do. Nate wants to join us."

Destiny blinked. "Wait. Someone else you know can shift into something, too?"

Rafe nodded. "A few of my deputies are wolf shifters as well. We have a pack of us who protect our witch community in the area."

"Were the murders to kill witches?" She looked wide-eyed at Kinsley.

"None of the victims were witches, that we know of." Rafe emptied his glass. "I guess it's a good thing you saw what you did today. The tissue samples of a witch or warlock would definitely be different than those of a mortal. Which is where you would come in. This is why I need you to talk with us. Now you understand *the why* should you ever run across any strange tissue slides that you look at."

"Wow. This is all mind-blowing. My bosses would think I'm nuts if I couldn't identify something in a sample. What are we looking for?"

"I have no idea. That's why *you're* here." Rafe looked like he was hoping Destiny could find an answer. Kinsley watched the way he dealt with her friend and tried not to read more into it, but her heart was losing when the suspicion crept into her mind.

Destiny looked around the table at each of them. Kinsley could see her mind swimming with questions. "I'd love to take a tissue sample from each of you to compare them to a normal sample, but that would have to be done in a hospital situation. I'm not sure we could do that without raising questions of why we're doing it."

Kinsley chimed in. "Which is why we need to stop whoever is committing these murders before one of our own ends up on your tissue slide and the government steps in to do more checking."

Destiny nodded, took a long pull from her glass and continued. "I can see why all of this is causing *you* guys to be nervous and why you've called me in. I've seen odd samples come through, but I've been able to find an explanation as to why. But now, if for some reason I can't find an answer, I'll have to call one of you before I tell my superiors. Damn it! This all sounds pretty dangerous for you."

Kai cracked the seal on the new whiskey, filled his tumbler, and passed the bottle to Rafe. Before refilling his, he checked with Kinsley, filled hers, and filled the glass Destiny held out, and then his own.

Kinsley nodded a thank you to Rafe, then turned to Destiny. "We've been friends since college, but I guess I never asked what it is you do every day. Wow. You've got a pretty important job, hon."

"I really do, and I love it. Being able to find organs for those who so badly need them is rewarding. We can also match muscle, skin, and ligaments for surgery for those who need it, and skin for burn victims. Those items can be stored for later use. Organs, on the other hand, have a time limit on them."

"Our victims have all been missing organs when we find them." Rafe glanced at Kai. "We have to find the killer before another individual ends up a victim."

"We can call Nate and head toward Ravensville tonight, I'm game. I'm ready to find this person. I've not had any new alarms on the Stingray, but I'll check before we head out tonight."

"Stingray?" Kinsley had never heard of anything like that besides a car and a fish.

Kai gave her a sexy smile. "It's a machine that acts like a cell tower for cell phones. We can pinpoint a location pretty close to where the users are, or were, at the time of a call. Just one of the neat things I get to do as a Special Agent investigator."

Kinsley swirled her glass with no ice. She got up to get some, hoping to defer the look she wanted to give Kai for being so secretive about where he's been for the past twenty-five years. "Anyone else need ice?"

They all agreed so she just pulled out the bin and took it to the table with a cup to make it easy to get the ice out of the bin. When glasses were full, she took it back to the freezer.

When she returned to the table, Rafe had Nate on the phone, and they'd planned a meet-up so they guys could go to Ravensville.

Rafe finished his phone call and laid it on the table. He looked at Kinsley. "Nate said something about Morgan seeing a vision in her mirror. He'll fill me in when he meets up with us. We're heading out about eleven."

Kinsley turned her attention to Kai as her stomach knotted, but she needed to know. "Down at the beach, you said something about mate-violence to Rafe. I have no idea what that means."

She looked from Rafe, back to Kai. "I want an answer. From either one of you, I don't care. What does that mean?"

Both guys looked at each other with a sternness she hadn't seen before. At the same time, a rumble went through the cabin, not once, but twice.

"Kins...that isn't called for. Stay calm." Rafe tipped his head down and glanced up at Kinsley.

Destiny flattened her hands on the table and looked around at each of them. "Was that an earthquake? I felt that!"

Without taking his eyes off Kinsley, Rafe answered her. "No, that would be caused by your best friend's abilities. When she's pissed, the world knows."

Kai laughed out loud. "Well, that explains a few things for me."

Kinsley didn't find either of them funny and set down her glass harder than she planned, but too bad. "What does mate-violence have to do with shifters?"

Kai ran his fingers through his silky-looking blonde hair that always seemed to lay perfect and looked at Rafe. "This is on *you* to explain to her. I gather the two of you already have a relationship, and I'm not stepping into the middle of *that*."

He looked back at Kinsley. "Shifters mate for life. When one realizes they've found a mate, the inner animal takes over and doesn't stop until they're mated."

Destiny threw her arms into the air. "And now I'm totally lost, so I'm even more curious. I still can't believe either of you can shift into an animal at will."

Rafe squirmed in his chair and leaned back. "Anger usually pre-empts a shift and that's what happened today. I don't like other men around women who I feel close to, and he just happened to be in the wrong place at the wrong time."

Destiny sat back. "He wasn't doing anything except talking to us!"

Rafe shrugged. "Mate-violence happens when a shifter mate is compromised or in danger. I didn't have control over my inner wolf this afternoon when I saw him near both of you." He turned to Kai. "Sorry about that. I certainly didn't mean to go at you that way."

Kinsley took in a deep breath and shook her head. "But...he asked you who *you* were protecting so hard, and you couldn't answer him!" Another rumble happened. Then she pointed at Kai. "And *you* were way too angry that he might have been protecting Destiny!" Kinsley turned her glare on Rafe. "So, which one of us is it?"

Rafe put his face in his hands.

Betrayal hit her like a tidal wave.

Kinsley grabbed her drink and pushed her chair back so hard that it fell over when she stood up. Her heart seared with pain. She stormed out the back door, wanting to get away from both men. She realized she deserved that reaction from Rafe. Had she given him her heart, none of this would be an issue, but right now, love was too much to deal with.

Standing near the porch rail furthest from the door, she stared out at the ocean, wishing life could wash away all of the bad happenings in her life as easily as it smoothed out the ripples in the sand. Too bad she couldn't drown in her whiskey!

How would I handle it if Rafe now wanted to be with Destiny?

How did I not see this coming?

She leaned against the corner post and stared out at the beach.

Chapter 7

When someone grabbed Kinsley's arm, she instinctively pulled away. In a blurred rush of movement, warm hands suddenly cupped her face and pulled her close as she tried to fight whoever it was. The possessive look in Kai's eyes couldn't be ignored as he stared at her. He claimed her mouth in a kiss so deep and fierce that she couldn't breathe. He scooped her tongue into his mouth, and the kiss was even better than when they were teenagers.

Hotter and more passionate...and full of a need that matched her own. Goddess it'd been far too long.

Kinsley dropped her glass and wrapped her arms around Kai's waist. Her fingers touched every corded muscle in his back; they were so hard it shocked her. His deep kiss sent sparks to her center that she hadn't felt in years, even with Rafe.

He pulled from the kiss and touched his forehead to hers, catching his breath in the process. "Damn it, Kins. This isn't how I wanted things to go between us right now, but..."

Her eyes were still closed, cherishing every memory of his kiss.

She had no words but heard every one of his. "When he came at me, I recognized the mate instinct in him. I wasn't sure which one of you he was protecting, but I saw the way he's been looking at Destiny since we've come back from the fight."

She still couldn't speak. The confusion of the last few minutes, and the realization of what was taking place, stabbed her in the heart.

He leaned away, his hands still holding her face, and she looked at him. His blue eyes were killing her, and the memories of their past came to the front of her mind. *Why have I never reached out to him?*

"Last week, when I saw you in the Dragon's Lair, I nearly took you over my shoulder and back to my room that day. You are *my* mate, *not* his, and I'll fight to the death for you. He just better not push it that far again." His thumb caressed her lower lip.

She searched his face, unsure of how to proceed. "I haven't heard from you in twenty-five years. My heart can't take breaking again if you leave one more time."

"I'm here now, babe. Don't shut me out."

She shook her head, denying his words. "I'm not your mate. You're a loner, Kai. I can't do this again..." She closed her eyes, unable to deal with the hurt looking back at her.

"Look at me...my feelings for you have never wavered, and I've never mated for life. I may have been with other women, but none of them get to me the way you do. I can't tell you how often you were in my dreams. This past week has been hell not knowing where I could find you!"

She laid her head on his chest, unable to find the words that could match what he just told her. Her heart broke and rejoiced at the same time. His arms wrapped around her, and he kissed her hair. Kinsley could only hold him tight, praying they would find time to sort all of this out.

Kai whispered in her ear as he massaged her back. "I don't think you need to worry about

Rafe or Destiny. I know the mating look when I see it. He's got it bad, but at the same time, I know what he feels for you. I'll give him time."

Kinsley leaned back enough to meet his gaze. "How can things be so messed up? This is uncomfortable right now, even for how bad I want to stay right here in your arms. I don't know if I can trust you to stick around."

The screen door squeaked, and Kinsley nearly jumped out of her skin. Destiny rushed into Kinsley's arms. "Oh Des. What a mess this is." Tears slid down Kinsley's face.

Destiny squeezed her tight. "Rafe feels awful. I'm not sure how I feel, but can we all sit down and figure this out? Please?"

Kinsley squeezed her eyes shut, not wanting to talk at all right now, but knew they had to make sense of it all. She pulled from Destiny. "Stay out here with Kai. I'll go talk to him." She glanced up at Kai. "I hope this won't take long."

* * * * *

Rafe paced in the kitchen, trying to control his anxiety as he massaged his neck and the knotted muscles. He knew that he'd just done to Kinsley exactly what Kai had done to her years ago, and he hated himself right now. When Kai ran after Kinsley on the back porch, Rafe had hugged Destiny, which led to a kiss like he'd never had before. Her body had molded against his as though they were made for one another, and now, he couldn't admit that he regretted it.

Destiny had pulled back, not from disgust, but from worry that Kinsley would see them. She wanted to go find her best friend on the porch.

Now, standing alone, he felt like an ass. *You can't love two people at the same time!* Yet he did, and maybe now understood Kinsley a bit more. Although he'd never felt that he'd found his mate in her, he still loved her hard. He'd never meant to hurt her, but as hard as he wanted it to work, there was a disconnect between them that wasn't all on her. The surprising connection he found with Destiny had shocked him as much as it had Destiny. It was different than what he felt for Kinsley.

His attack on Kai needed to be dealt with also. His own reactions had gone haywire fast.

When the screen door squeaked opened, he knew that he'd take whatever got thrown at him. Kai had a right to come at him again if he wanted. Kinsley could certainly incinerate him on the spot. He deserved it. Expecting to see Kai, Rafe was shocked as he turned to see Kinsley step inside alone and stand behind a kitchen chair. The tears in her eyes and the broken expression he saw tore his chest open.

She didn't say a word, only made eye contact with him as though she could see into his mind.

How long they stared at each other, he couldn't say. Then she closed her eyes and tipped her head down. Her shoulders shook as she cried, but her fingers fisted, and he prepared for whatever she'd do to him as his muscles knotted even more, waiting for her wrath.

The cabin shook twice.

He waited.

Nothing, but he never took his eyes off of Kinsley as he braced himself for more repercussions.

When she looked back up at him, the agony in her gaze was the worst thing he'd ever experienced. He wished he could relieve her pain. "I deserve whatever you have to say about me. Kins, I never planned for things to go this way."

She nodded. "If I had only opened my heart wide enough, you wouldn't have had to look any further. It's *my* fault, and I'll take the blame." She moved around to sit in a chair at the table and he joined her. Her hand reached toward him, and he took it. "Kai and I had a relationship in high school. He is the reason my heart has been closed off for so many years. Rafe, I'm so sorry."

He looked into her eyes that still sparkled through her tears, like green gems in the gentle rain. "There's nothing to be sorry for, hon. Fate has stepped in to correct everything, I suppose." He squeezed her hand in his. "You told me from the beginning that you couldn't commit to us. I hoped I could change your mind, but now you and Kai can begin again."

Kinsley took in a few jagged breaths. "Maybe. I have a lot of shit to process before that can happen. He never tried to reach me, and all of this time, he's been a loner. Men don't change. As far as Destiny is concerned, she'll be true to you forever if the two of you move forward." She bit her lower lip. "You both have my blessing, Rafe." The flow of tears came rough and full as she laid her head in her hands while her body shook with each sob, ripping his heart as he watched her.

He stood up and pulled her with him to hold her as she cried. If he could go back twenty-four hours, would he want anything changed? The memory of their last night together will forever be in his head, in a special place reserved only for Kinsley. Rafe rubbed her back, his fingers feeling the knots along her spine. "You know I loved you, Kins. We both tried to make it work. If it helps at all, Kai has my blessing to be with you. I hope the two of you can work out the years of misunderstandings between you. He seems like a good man."

Kinsley's chest burned like hell, as if she'd been struck with a fireball. The pain of losing someone so close, then rediscovering Kai after so many years, was more than she could handle today. She held tight to Rafe's muscular body, hating that they would no longer be a couple, but her heart never gave him a chance. He was handsome beyond belief, yet she'd refused to open her heart to him.

She pulled back to look up at him, snapped in a few tissues for her nose, and had so much she wanted to say. The words wouldn't come out right now, but she read his eyes as easily as ever before. He'd been so good to her. She didn't deserve him, or his friendship, yet hoped they would all still be friends.

Rafe tried to speak but she put two fingers over his soft lips. She wanted to get her words out before he spoke.

Losing Destiny's friendship would kill her for sure. Trying to stay calm enough to talk, Kinsley pressed her lips together for a moment. "I need to talk to Des. Goddess, what happened here today? Everything happened at once. She saw things she has never seen before, Rafe. For her to actually witness you two shifting, Danteleon coming out of the water as that horrid creature and seeing me toss fireballs like it was a softball game!"

She looked up when the screen door squeaked open.

"Are you two alright in here?" Destiny peered in.

Kinsley stepped away from Rafe. "I need a drink. This day will go down as the most insane day ever for all of us." She waved her hand, and another bottle of whiskey appeared.

Destiny and Kai cautiously stepped back into the kitchen. Destiny sat in the same chair from earlier. "Here's my glass. I'll drink one with you. What time is it anyway?"

Kai checked his watch. "Three pm. Holy shit! Count me in, too." He stepped next to Kinsley and tipped her face up to his with a finger beneath her chin. "Are you okay, babe?"

She blinked away tears, met his gaze and nodded, unable to say a word after meeting his look of passion and caring. He kissed her forehead, checked Rafe for any reaction, and saw that he was whispering to Destiny. Relief washed over her that there wouldn't be another outbreak because he dared to kiss her in front of Rafe.

Kinsley pushed a half glass of whiskey toward Kai and Rafe, then poured some for her and Destiny. She sat down and stared into her drink, knowing there was so much she wanted to say to her best friend. "Des, I know you must have a million questions in your head. I'm not sure where you want to start but just spit out whatever you need to know."

She met Destiny's beautiful blue eyes and instantly hoped she felt something for Rafe. "I won't lie. I had no idea that my being here would create such a mess today."

Rafe reached out for Destiny's hand, and she took his. "None of this is your fault. Understand that. Events today happened because evil knocked at our door. That creature could easily have manipulated everything that happened, from my attack on Kai, to you seeing Kinsley's magic, and the two of us shifting. No mortal has ever witnessed me during a shift. I'm sorry you had to see that without any warning."

Kinsley reached out for Kai, and he reciprocated. Their discussion and explanations helped Destiny understand more about their world, but Kinsley knew it would take more than one night of talking.

Two hours later, Kai checked his watch. "We have a few hours before we meet Nate at the station. I want to talk with Kins next door."

Rafe also checked his watch. "Sure."

Kai nodded, then squeezed Kinsley's hand. "Will you be safe if you stay here with Destiny tonight after we leave? I'm not sure what the protection is here, but I don't want that asshole coming back out of the water after you."

Feeling a bit better after their discussion, Kinsley nodded. "Wards are a magical veil with perimeters that he can't get through, no matter what he does. We reinforce them every thirty days." Destiny frowned at her. "I'd love to spend the night here with you. We have a lot more to cover."

Destiny nodded. "I'd love that. Am I the only hungry one here?"

Kinsley finally laughed for the first time in hours. "I think I can whip us up something to eat before the guys leave." She hoped the tension would ease, but she wasn't sure how. "I can conjure some rib steaks. I think we all need some time to digest the day's events."

Just saying the words made her relax. The others appeared to be relieved, too. Kinsley waved her arm over the table and a full steak dinner for four appeared, steaming hot with a baked potato and veggies.

Kai just shook his head. "It'll take me a while to get used to that!"

Not much got discussed over dinner, but thoughts bounced around in her own head. She hugged Destiny after dinner. "I'll be back in a few hours. You two need time to talk and so do we." Kinsley and Kai went next door where she knew they could be alone.

* * * * *

In Nate's backyard, Morgan excelled at everything Jadis was teaching her and Logan. Pride in the way he learned and performed the tasks Jadis showed him made Morgan happy. Because of Jadis, the two of them could now use magick in better ways when they had to deal with the dark warlock. Certainly, calling him the demon was the same thing. Morgan hated the man and the control he thought he had over them.

Jadis had taught them how to conceal themselves from anyone should the need arise. Mortals would not detect them, nor the evil entities with the spells she showed them. The day had flown by, and she couldn't believe it was now mid-afternoon.

"Your family grimoire has more spells and how to perfect them. Of course, it will take practice, and I suggest you both do them together. Always use white candles, salt your circle of protection, and pray for your safety to the goddess before every spell."

Logan grabbed his ringing cell phone on the outdoor table, excused himself, and answered it. He'd stepped away from Morgan, so she took that time to thank Jadis. "I'll be sure to let my parents know how much help you're giving to Logan and I. We do appreciate it."

"We have so much more in the grimoire regarding spells. Let's get together next week, back here. You both have a lot to cram in." Jadis checked her phone calendar and suddenly went silent. She turned toward the ocean and looked out over the waves as if scanning for danger. "Something has happened today. I can feel it." Jadis turned back to Morgan. "If you use your scrying mirror, you might see what it was. Keep me posted. I have to go. I'll be back next week."

With that, Jadis disappeared. Morgan turned to see Logan smiling as he talked on the phone. She assumed it was Mandy and headed inside to give him privacy. She found Nate in their workout room. He had a few huge pieces of equipment with weights and pulleys, and he smiled at her as she stood in the doorway. Sweat beaded over his muscular shoulders and neck, not to mention his forehead.

"Hey, handsome." Morgan tossed him his towel. "I love watching you work out."

Nate wiped his face and leaned in for a quick kiss. "I need a shower. I hope your day was productive with Jadis."

"It was." She followed him into the kitchen to refill his water jug just as Logan came in from the pool area.

"That call was from the veterinarian, Mom! Nate, thank you for putting a word in for me. I got the job! He wants me to stop by in a few days to show me around." Logan shook Nate's hand. "He said getting my license would fit right into his plans for bringing an intern on staff. Wow, that sounds strange, but I guess I am a vet...or will soon be one! My testing date can't be too far away. I just want it over."

Morgan hugged her son. "I couldn't be prouder of the man you're becoming. You've worked hard and done your studies. Working with animals has always mattered to you. It's a great fit."

"If Nate hadn't put in a word for me, I doubt I would have gotten my foot in the door." Logan grabbed a glass, filled it with ice and water. He suddenly pressed his palm to the countertop, tipped his head sideways, and looked back at Morgan. "Can you feel that, Mom?"

"Feel what?" Morgan thought it strange that Jadis felt something and now Logan mentioned it. Why couldn't she feel that something had happened to the atmosphere?

Logan shook it off. "Something isn't right. I don't know what, but it's like a premonition. Jadis said I need to pay more attention when I sense that. I'm going back to the apartment tonight. I have to keep reading the grimoire. There's so much I need to learn. Should I bring it back here tomorrow or do you want it left there?" Logan took a long drink from his glass.

Morgan glanced at Nate.

He shrugged a shoulder. "That's your call, babe. Do you want it here?"

She wasn't sure. "I think if my mirror shows me something, it might be important to have the grimoire here."

Nate's phone buzzed, and he picked it up. "It's a message from Rafe. We're heading to Ravensville tonight at eleven. He wants me to meet him and Kai at the station and go from there."

The look Logan gave her sent a chill down her spine.

Morgan looked at Nate and back at Logan. "I saw a body in my mirror yesterday. It was at the bottom of a ravine, but I couldn't see the exact location."

"You think it's another murder, Mom?"

She met Nate's gaze as an eerie feeling crept through her system. "Let's hope not. Please be careful tonight. Keep our connection open so I know what's going on. Please?" Ever since they'd been together, she could feel his thoughts and feelings, as he could hers.

"My connection with you is always open." He kissed her forehead. "I'm heading to the shower, then I'll call Rafe and see what's up."

Morgan watched him rip off his tank top as he headed toward their wing of the house. She would never tire of admiring his body, and her cheeks warmed in front of Logan.

"I love that he makes you happy, Mom. You deserve that." He gave her a hug. "I'm off to the apartment. Last night I hated to put the grimoire down. Mandy's enjoying the history, too. It scares her to think if we stay together, that our children will likely have powers, but with the two of us having abilities, I think it's a given."

"It is. You just won't know at what age they'll *show* their abilities. Stay alert on your way over there. Maybe you should just teleport until we know the demon is behind bars and without his powers. I need to contact my dad to see if he's heard any news. Be careful."

Chapter 8

After Logan left, Morgan couldn't resist the pull to look into her mirror. She sat down at her desk, closed her eyes, and grounded herself. Once the peacefulness surrounded her and she knew her white light protected her, she pulled off the black velvet that covered the mirror. Placing her hands palms down on each side of the mirror, she waited, concentrating on the happenings of the day and why she had never felt the disturbance that Jadis and Logan tuned in to.

Only her image looked back at her from the black mirror.

Morgan's eyes scanned the blackness from top to bottom, side to side. "Where is the location of the body I saw the other day? Mirror, show me where to find the body."

Then in the upper left corner, swirling color began to remove the black and replace it with a highway. An old house sat on the right side of the road.

Not being from this area, Morgan didn't recognize it!

"Nate! Are you out of the shower yet? Come here!" As she continued watching, it was as though she viewed a video. Slowly another road on the left passed by, but the next road came into view. The mirror stopped, then showed the deep ravine she'd seen the other day.

The moment Nate put his hand on her shoulder, she glanced up to make sure he saw it. A sense of doom spread through her as she watched, red clouds took over the mirror, and a creature appeared. The mirror zoomed in. Jagged teeth like she'd never seen before visualized and soon the face took up the entire space.

The creature tipped back its head and let out an eerie laugh. When it looked back, directly into her eyes, Morgan gasped. The creature then looked directly up at Nate, and back to Morgan. "Beware when you walk the dark woods. You won't be alone!"

Another laughing howl, and the mirror went black.

"Holy shit!" Nate tossed the black cover over the mirror. "I'm glad I saw that, or I might not have believed it. I need to call Rafe."

"Hon, before that, I saw a highway with an old house off to the right. The mirror passed one road, but stopped at the second, then went directly to the deep ravine I saw the other day. Is that enough to tell you where to look?"

Nate dialed the phone as he nodded to her, and he put the phone on speaker.

Rafe answered. "Hey, thanks for calling back. We've had some shit go down today over at the cabins. I'm not sure I can even explain it all. Let me know if you can be at the station by ten. We can go over everything with Kai then, before we head north."

"Morgan just shut down her scrying mirror. She saw a few directions and the deep ravine again. Before the mirror went black, a nasty creature appeared right in her face with teeth like I've never seen before. It told us to beware of walking in the dark woods. We wouldn't be alone!"

"Shit! I saw that creature come out of the water and walk toward the shore today. Kai and

I attack it, but it dove under water and got away. What the hell?”

“Morgan’s already dialing her parents. She said they need to know about this.”

Morgan held her phone to her ear. “I’m calling Jadis next to let her know!”

As Nate walked toward the office door, she heard his last question to Rafe. “Is everyone okay?”

Morgan’s mother answered. “Is dad there with you? Things are happening here and I’m sure it’s *Danteleon*! He just appeared in my scrying mirror, and he showed himself to Rafe today. Rafe attacked him, but he got away by diving into the ocean. Have either of you felt anything?”

“Your father must have because he teleported directly to the Witch’s Council.”

“I’m living at Nate’s now, but I can meet you at my apartment above the bookstore. Get there as soon as you can. We think there’s another body out there somewhere. It’s being used to lure the guys into the woods.”

“Your father just reached out to me. He said to have Logan available. You’re going to need his powers tonight. Your father said he's the only one who can carry out this task."

"Mom, we don't even know what his abilities are yet!"

"You don't need to know what he can do. The abilities will come forward when he needs them. Just have him with you, dear. We'll let you know when we're coming through."

Morgan laid her phone down as Nate came back into her office after talking with Rafe. His muscles bulged at his neck and shoulders, and his eyes filled with emotion. She knew something wasn't right. "What happened with Rafe?"

"I don't even know where to start. Ummm, Kinsley's friend, Destiny, arrived at the cabins today. She does the tissue testing at the center in Portland. Apparently she is mortal and had no idea about witches or shifters until...she saw it first-hand with her own eyes! Shit hit the fan, and they're trying to keep her calm. What a mess!"

"She saw Rafe shift?"

Nate nodded. "He and Kai shifted, Kai's a cougar shifter, and both attacked the creature, but he ran back into the ocean and disappeared. Destiny watched the whole thing. She also saw Kinsley throw fireballs at the creature and watched him start on fire. At the same time, Kinsley's anger burned a circle around her out in the grass."

"Shit. Not good for a mortal to witness. I know that much. Poor Kinsley."

"I'll know more when I get to the station. They want to shift and look around in Ravensville. I know exactly where that second road is on the left. What you saw in the mirror should be back there in the woods."

"My parents are meeting me at the book store. Dad specifically stated that Logan was to go with you guys tonight to help against *him!* You know how dangerous he can be. I'm so tired of this!"

Nate pulled her up into his arms, and she held on tight. It was her fault the danger was coming after her friends. If she had just agreed to go with Danteleon that night at the beach, none of this would be happening.

He whispered against her ear. "I can hear those thoughts, babe. Stop."

She leaned back to look at him. "I'm the one he wants, yet he'll kill all of you in order to get to me. Is it worth that?"

Nate gently gripped her shoulders. "We're not discussing that again. Your father is going to learn what needs to be done to get him back in jail. Don't put yourself at risk by driving anywhere. Please just teleport until we know what's going on." He held her again and kissed her hair.

Just running her fingers over the strength in his back gave Morgan strength of her own. She had to stay positive and not let the evil invade her thoughts and make her weak.

Concentrate on the positive!

* * * * *

Logan sat at his mom's old apartment with the grimoire. He'd popped a beer from the fridge and turned the old parchment pages, careful not to tear them as he went through the ancient book. The electricity that had tingled his skin while he trained with Jadis today still concerned him. He'd never had that sensation before, and knew he needed to find answers. They had to be within these pages somewhere.

The protector's identity wasn't something he wanted but apparently, he had no choice. The ability and title passed on to every other generation. *Why had my grandfather never spoken to me about it when he knew this was a possibility?*

Mandy would be here soon. He wanted her to learn along with him, and hoped she found her family grimoire. Logan gulped the first beer and went into the kitchen for another, hoping it would help him be less angry with the whole situation.

Before he reached the refrigerator, an apparition of a man appeared in the hallway beyond the kitchen. Logan put his hand on the back of a chair for balance. He blinked and shook his head, but the apparition stood still. *Is this what happens when I read the grimoire?* Nothing had ever appeared to him before.

The old man wore a dark brown cloak with a hood hanging in the back, his gray hair long and straggly, and his gnarled fingers held onto a rod made of a tree limb for walking. His light eyes peered from an ancient face that had seen too many battles.

"My son…do not be afraid. *You* are the chosen one. I'm here to guide you."

Logan rubbed his eyes, thankful that Mandy hadn't shown up. She'd freak out at this. Or maybe not. Maybe she's seen apparitions. They'd never discussed it. Logan stepped closer and tipped his head at the old man.

"My name is Dreas. I have been with your family for over five hundred years. I know about your lineage, my son."

"Why am I just now finding out about you?"

The old man took in a long, tired breath. "The more you read, the more you learn. I cannot fix the past."

Logan knew he needed another beer. "What are you?"

His walking stick gently tapped the floor three times. "I am here to help you understand what's coming and to guide you in the right direction."

Logan touched his ring and turned it on his finger. *Mom! I'm in your apartment. I need you now!*

I'm coming, Logan!

The air behind Logan rippled and a hand touched his shoulder. "Oh my!"

Logan didn't look back at his mother, afraid the apparition would disappear. "Do you see him?"

Her fingers tightened on his collar bone. "I do. Damn."

"This is Dreas. He said I should read about him in the grimoire. He's been in our family for five-hundred years."

Morgan stepped closer to Logan, then spoke to the old man. "Why are you here? This is *my* son. What do you want?"

The old man's eyes never wavered. "I am here as a guide for Logan as he learns his path. Evil is coming, and he needs to be strong and ready."

Logan turned to his mother. "That is what Jadis keeps telling me. That I need to be strong. What the hell is going on, Mom?"

"We need to read more. There are so many pages. We've put off reading for too long. If my parents had only warned me years ago what we might be up against!" Morgan's fingers rubbed her tree of life amulet. *Mom, Logan and I are in my old apartment. Get here soon and bring Dad!*

The old man spoke with a gravelly voice. "You will come into abilities beyond your wildest dreams that will be used to protect those you love. You must learn how and when to use them so keep reading. I will return." With a slight breeze, the old man disappeared.

Logan opened the fridge, grabbed a beer, and downed half of it in one gulp. "Do *you* see apparitions? This one is my first. I'm not liking any of this, Mom, just so you know. It would have been nice to have a choice in what's happening!" He raked his fingers back through his hair, as he looked around the kitchen and down the hallway. "Will I know when he's coming back? Or will he just show up when I'm out on the street one day?"

"Hon, I don't think so. If he said he's here to be your guide, I'm guessing he'll show up when you're alone somewhere, most likely your place or here. You were alone, and the grimoire is here." His mother opened a bottle of wine she'd left, obviously just for this purpose.

"I'm glad Mandy wasn't here to see that. She would have freaked out. I wonder if she sees apparitions. This is all ridiculous!" He downed the rest of his beer and tossed the can in the trash. He could have sworn he heard Mandy's voice, yet when he looked around, there was no sign of her.

"What are you looking for?" Morgan leaned against the kitchen counter with her glass in her hand.

Logan shook his head. "This entire day has been like a dream, beginning with what Jadis taught us about cloaking our presence and sending out our powers to destroy shit, to seeing ghosts, and hearing voices."

"He wasn't a ghost. Well, okay, sort of." Morgan raised her brows at him.

Logan waved his hand in the air. "And I just heard Mandy ask if I was alright."

"Son...you hear her because of your connection, which means you two have found each other as mates. That's how it works. Your souls are connected. Have you felt her feelings or thoughts before?"

"I guess I have. It's just weird." Logan shook his head. Another beer got pulled from the fridge as he tried to make sense of the information swirling through his brain like a wind storm.

This is insane.

Who can do magick?

His mom reached out to hug him. "Both of our lives have gotten weird. I don't think we can change who we are now. When you see Dreas next time, be ready with a few questions that only he can answer. Let's go read some pages until your grandparents get here."

Logan led the way over to the couch where the grimoire lay open on the coffee table, some pages were pulling away from the center, some corners crumbled and torn. He sat next to his mom, and as he reached for the book, the pages quickly turned themselves so that the book lay open to The Protectors and Guides section. He glanced at his mom. "What the hell?"

Another ripple in the air pulled Logan's attention to the over-stuffed chair, and he saw an old woman holding a cup and saucer, sipping her tea. "Mom?"

Morgan tipped her head at the old woman. "Izzy. You could warn me when you're going to arrive."

"You've seen her before?" Now there was no way he could say his life was normal. That had gone out the window after graduation when he moved to this strange area with his mother. *At least I have Mandy who doesn't think I'm nuts.*

Morgan took in a breath. "Yes. She frightened me the first time I saw her here in this apartment."

Izzy let out a high-pitched cackle. "I'm sorry to barge in, but the old wizard, Dreas, advised me that I should stop in."

Logan sat back on the sofa. "Oh my gosh! Now I've heard everything. Ghosts who talk to each other about us, then stop in to warn us about shit they already know is going to happen. The two of you could zap the evil and be done with it, right?"

As though on cue, with another ripple in the air, Logan stared at his grandparents, Annette and Callan Scott. They looked as though they just stepped from a photo shoot. Their clothing was pristine, and not a hair out of place. He knew he shouldn't be so cocky, but someone should have warned him his life would turn upside down after twenty-one.

Logan waved an arm in the air. "Hey, welcome to the party! I'm glad you could join us!" Logan set his beer on the side table and noticed Izzy had disappeared. He turned back to his grandparents. "I hope you have some insight for us, since we seem to be trudging through this magickal world all on our own. I'd like to know more about the upcoming evil that I keep getting told about, yet no one has said what it is."

"Logan!" His mother put her hand on his thigh, likely hoping to calm him down.

His grandfather waved his hand, and two chairs appeared for them to sit in. Logan tried to stay calm so he could understand once they started explaining things. There should be a school he could have attended to learn all of this like a normal warlock. "If I ever have children, you can bet that I won't let them be ignorant of the possible abilities they might have."

His grandfather nodded. "That is certainly something you need to consider. Depending on who you mate with, if they have abilities, the chances of your children also having abilities is even greater. As is the chance that *your* first grandson will also be a Protector. This skips a generation, and we all handle it differently. The section you have open will tell you more, but the Protectors have powers that other witches and warlocks don't have, along with other inherited abilities."

"I need to know *when* these are going to show up." Logan raked his hair back in frustration.

Callan leaned forward to rest his forearms on his knees and looked at Logan. "Son, my hope is that you learn about the abilities before you need to use them. So far that's not happened. Tonight, you must accompany Nate and Rafe when they go to Ravensville to investigate a body drop. Your mother has seen where the site is in her scrying mirror and relayed that to Nate, but the dark warlock also came through her mirror and told them not to roam the dark woods alone."

Logan's nervous system seemed to be electrified as his breathing became strained and heat radiated throughout his body. When he closed his eyes, he saw a vision like never before as something rampaged through the woods toward him, and he opened his eyes. His fingers grabbed onto his mother's thigh, and he stared at her as he pointed to his head. "You saw this?"

She nodded. "You are the only one who can deal with this should it appear while Nate and Rafe are out there tonight. There's not much time. They are meeting at the station at ten tonight. Your powers will be stronger than mine. It has to be you. Nate and Rafe have no magickal abilities other than shifting and sensing danger."

Logan stared at his grandfather. "Do I get a warning of what's waiting for us?"

"I wish I could tell you. Danteleon can take any form he chooses." Callan picked up a velvet bag he'd brought with him, and he pulled out a wide metal neck shackle that locked in the back. "This will stop all of his powers once this is placed around his neck. Your abilities will magickally make it as big as it needs to be once it's in your hands. When you connect these ends together, your abilities will help it seal itself, only to be removed by the Witch's Council. We will *all* be safe once this is done."

Logan stared at the ceiling, his mind reeling from the possibilities of death for all of them. *What if I fail? What if Nate dies because of me?* He looked over at his mother and shook his head.

"You have to go with them tonight." She nearly begged him to go.

Logan glanced at his grandfather and looked deep into the eyes that were so like his own. "Do I have a guarantee this will work? Or do I die with the rest of them?"

"Hopefully, no one will die...but *your* presence will be necessary. I'm sorry your first test as Protector is so extreme." Callan put the ancient shackle back in the bag and handed it to Logan. "Once that is connected, you only need to think of me there, and I'll meet you to return him to the council. Their jail is made of special iron bars, the same material as the neck shackle. Once he's in their jail, his powers are useless."

As soon as Logan touched the bag, the weight of the magick traveled through his fingers and into his muscles. The strength went through every fiber and his clothes tightened. "Shit!"

His grandfather watched. "That's how some of this happens. We can't explain it. Jadis can guide you and so can Dreas. I understand he made a visit today."

"Oh, he was here!" Logan picked up his beer and finished it. "A warning before his appearance would have been nice, like maybe showing up in a dream first!" He stood up and pulled his phone from his pocket. "I need to talk to Mandy before I go anywhere. I'll be right back." He walked down the hallway to the back bedroom for privacy and was about ready to pull his hair out because of the way others seemed to be controlling his life.

Mandy answered her phone. "Something's happening with you. I can feel it. You have me worried."

Just hearing her voice calmed him somewhat. "I'm glad you didn't come to mom's apartment yet. Things *are* happening. I guess I can call it a *mission* that I have to go on tonight according to my grandfather. I'll call you as soon as I get back, but it'll be in the middle of the night. Whatever this evil is, it's rearing its head in the woods in Ravensville. I'm not sure when or how this will go down but cross your fingers that we all stay safe."

"I will be awake until I hear from you. Just call, no matter what time. I love you, Logan. Be safe."

"I love you, too. I'll call you later." He hung up, surprised at the feelings for Mandy that had grown so strong since he'd moved here. They tried to spend time together, but her job and his had gotten in the way, and once he started at the vet's office, their time together would be even less. He fisted his hands in anger, and the entire building shook. He looked around for crumbling stone or cracks in the wall but saw none.

"Logan!"

He rolled his eyes. "I'm fine, Mom. I'll be right there."

"My parents are gone, hon. Please stay calm," she called out from the kitchen.

He breathed out a relaxing breath. Now he could talk with his mom and not have them hearing. Back in the kitchen, she waited at the counter and set down her empty glass. He couldn't handle the look of sadness in her eyes and reached out to scoop her close.

Logan hadn't realized how tiny his mother actually was...or had the magick made him taller and bigger in an instant. "I'll do my best tonight, I promise. I love you."

"I know you'll be safe, but it won't be without danger. Be careful and keep your senses up. Don't forget the black bag."

"I'll put it in my backpack, so I don't forget it tonight."

Chapter 9

Kinsley walked into Kai's cabin with him right behind her, hoping they could make sense of what happened on the porch. He closed and locked the door, then leaned against it and put his head back. Looking at the ceiling, he took a deep breath, and she almost felt it through her own body.

Their gazes met from across the room, and the sexual tension between them made it hard to think. The crystal blue of his eyes appeared to have tiny ice chips in them. Having him this close, with memories of their last meeting at the Dragon's Lair, seemed to be melting her anger toward him, as was her heart.

Finally, alone with him, she had time to get her head together as she admired Kai, standing tall, built, and so powerful. The veins in his neck and arms were visible over the sculpted muscles. How long would he stay? Would today be a one-day stand, and when it was over, she'd never see him again? Just like before? So many questions came at once. At least they had time alone right now; she needed to make the most of it.

Thinking back on his anger when he thought Rafe was protecting her as his mate...was his anger because *he* wanted her? *Could I get that lucky?* He'd admitted it in Destiny's cabin...*but was it true?*

His gaze held hers as though it were his arms wrapped around her. His jaw tightened. "Yes...Kins, it *is* true."

She searched his eyes and felt his need to her bones. His look stripped her naked and begged her to come closer. "How can you know what I'm thinking?"

Kai shrugged a shoulder. "I just do. It's there in my head. I know I have to re-earn your trust, but please know that I'll do whatever it takes to earn it back. I'm not going anywhere. I may have another job down the line, but I'll return here to you. I *have* nowhere to call home." He pushed away from the door, never breaking their gaze, and walked straight at her, as though his wounds didn't exist. She knew to be wary of the tenderness in his eyes.

Kinsley stood her ground, unsure of what he was going to do. If he tried to grab her again, she may have to respond with more magic to protect herself.

When he tenderly cupped her face, he stared into her eyes. "I can't believe I have you in my hands and that today isn't a dream ...again. You're warm and I can feel you. I've needed you for so many years that I can't even explain it." His mouth took hers, hungry passion, and hot, as his tongue ignited her senses.

Her knees weakened, and she gripped his taut forearms, but he held tight to her face, never breaking their kiss. A whimper slipped from her throat before he slowly pulled away. Their eyes reconnected like never before, and she thought she was drowning. She couldn't breathe. Butterflies flipped in her stomach. "Why do I feel sixteen again?"

His eyes searched her face. His words were slow and deliberate. "Because nothing has changed over time where our feelings are concerned. I love you more now than I did before, and I'm sorry for whatever happened that I lost you." He pulled her close, his strong arms embracing her in gentle comfort. "I don't ever want to let go of you. I'm afraid I won't find my way back. We have so much to talk about."

The heat of his chest pressed against her cheek. The beat of his heart raced in her ear. The love of her life had returned, but could it heal the crack in her heart? She had to work at it. She'd given Rafe hope for a future yet let him down. Kai was here with her, and she vowed to make it work this time. "Can we sit on the couch before you weaken my knees any further?"

"You go sit down. I'll get us a drink."

When he joined her, he sat at the end, pulled the ottoman close and put his bare feet up, then handed her a tumbler of bourbon. "I think we need this to get through all the questions we both have."

His arm went around her shoulders as she put her feet up next to his. Words needed to be said first, and she couldn't look at him while she spoke, so instead, swirled the ice in her glass. "I want you to know that Rafe could never break through the barrier I had built around my heart because of *you*. He was so good to me, he did everything right, yet I just couldn't give him what he needed. My heart breaks for him because he waited for me to commit for so many years."

Kai touched her foot with his. "And how is he going to deal with me being back in your life?"

She could feel the deepness of his voice vibrate through her body. When she looked up at him, love looked back. "He's already given us his blessing. He won't stand in your way." Kinsley waited for her words to sink in. "I just hope that he and Destiny can meet in the middle. I have no idea of her feelings for him. I think she may be seeing someone in Portland."

Kai chuckled. "From what I saw today, he'll make sure she knows how he feels about her. He may have to work a little to win her over, but when we find our mate, we know...through smell." Kai brushed a strand of her hair away from her face. "Just like I may have to work a little to win you again. I don't plan on giving up, Kins. You *are* my mate. My insides are clawing for me to take you but now is not the time for that. Just know, one day, I *will* claim you."

Kinsley shook her head. "Today was intense. I had no idea you were a shifter, too. This is insane."

Kai smiled at her, highlighting his handsome features and chiseled jawline. "No, what's insane is that you have abilities that a mortal only dreams about. That'll take a bit of getting used to for me. You could fry my ass in a heartbeat."

Her cheeks heated as she thought about her abilities. "I guess I could have. When I learned about it, I was shocked. My parents weren't sure we would have powers because my father is mortal. Kind of strange, but he accepted us for who we are. He loves that mom is a witch. Keeping it a secret is what is hard. Des had no idea about shifters, witches, and magick, so I need to explain that to her. Maybe Rafe will ease her into that. We'll see."

Kai set down his tumbler on the side table. "You are even more gorgeous than I remember. My dreams don't do you justice." With a finger beneath her chin, he turned her face toward him and tenderly kissed her.

A kiss that sent her stomach slithering to her toes and awakened her heart. His lips were warm and firm, demanding a response. Feelings from long ago came rushing back as though it were only yesterday that they were in love.

He ended the kiss with another light kiss on her lips. "I'll never get enough of you. You make my inner cougar want to race along the shoreline and tell everyone you belong to me."

Kinsley lay her head in the crook of his shoulder and draped a leg over his. "I've not been this happy in years. I don't know where to begin for us. One day at a time, but we have to get through tonight. I know you want to investigate Ravensville. I'll be at Destiny's cabin when you return. I doubt either of us will sleep tonight."

Talking with Kai made time fly as they caught up on each other's past and what they hoped for the future. She knew things wouldn't be easy, but there wasn't a hurry to put their relationship on track. They were already there. Getting to know each other all over again would be fun, learning the likes and dislikes, so they could meld as one. She hoped it would heal her trust issues.

Kai's phone vibrated from a text. He checked it. "Rafe is ready to head to the station. He's got news from Nate, who's meeting us there with Logan."

She sat forward. "Logan? I wonder why he's going with you guys. I'll text Morgan later and talk to her."

"I'll walk you over to Destiny's." Before he moved again, he kissed her one last time, pulling her onto his lap to hold her tight as his mouth took hers.

His urgency nearly equaled hers, and she couldn't wait for later. But an eerie foreboding crept into her senses. One she didn't like, and it made her worry about the night's events in Ravensville.

* * * * *

Rafe turned a light on over the kitchen sink, and sat back down at the table with Destiny, his mind more at ease than it had been all day. He'd finally found his mate and now truly knew what it felt like. When he should have a feeling of loss regarding Kinsley, having Destiny in his life brought sunshine and happiness for a future he hoped would be a bright one. Kinsley would always hold a special place in his heart. She'd tried to warn him that she couldn't commit, but he wouldn't listen. He should have felt the lack of connection between them. He wanted to be with someone so bad he couldn't sense it.

He and Destiny had spent hours talking about the day's events, the hows and the whys. "I hope explaining all of our abilities has helped you understand us witches and shifters. The demons after them are as real as the killer we're looking for."

Her light red hair covered her eyes as she entwined her fingers together. "I feel as though today was a dream like no other I've ever had. Like something one sees on TV or reads about in paranormal books. I won't lie and say that I'm okay with it all." She looked up and brushed her hair away from her face. Her blue eyes would forever be his downfall. "Can you assure me that you'll never shift in the middle of a conversation like that again? I doubt it."

His hand reached out to cover her fingers. "I can't, no. Depending on the circumstances, yes, it could happen again but know that it'll always be for your protection against whatever threat I'm facing."

"Is this something you have control over or no?" Her eyes pleaded with him to make her understand as she unfolded her fingers and threaded them through his.

"For the most part, yes, I can control it. I *can* say that in Kai's presence, it won't ever happen again. If he's truly the one Kinsley has been pining for since high school, I wish them the best. In my heart, I knew she would never be mine. It was just something I felt. The day I met you when you first came to Pebble Cove...I had a hard time not claiming you then. Woman...you have no idea how strong my feelings are for you even though we've just become friends. That's how it is with shifters...and we mate for life. When we meet our mate, we can smell it, and we just know."

She watched him as he tried to explain away his time with Kinsley. Would she go back to Portland and never return? He had no guarantee.

Destiny's thumb rubbed the back of his hand. "You know nothing about me, Rafe. How can you know you want me without knowing anything?"

"For shifters, we just know as soon as we smell our mate. I sensed you before I even pulled up in front of you and Kinsley when you last visited. It's that simple. You can deny our attraction if you like. I'll make it hard for you to do that, but I'll do my damnedest to make you see that we are meant to be together. You aren't married. I know that."

"No, nor am I romantically attached to anyone."

"See?"

Destiny closed her eyes and shook her head. "I don't know."

"Give us time. That's all I ask. I know you have to be in Portland, and I have to be here." Rafe's phone rang and Nate's photo came up. "I have to take this." He leaned back in his chair and opened the line.

Nate's voice came over the phone. "I hope it's not a bad time. We've had some weird things go on here today."

"Well, I think I've got you beat!" Rafe replied.

"Morgan had visions in her scrying mirror today regarding us in Ravensville tonight, so Logan is going with us."

Rafe leaned forward to rest his forearms on the table. "Logan has nothing to do with this investigation."

"The demon showed himself in Morgan's mirror today...after he allowed her to see where the latest body is. Then he appeared and told her we should be careful about walking in the dark woods alone tonight."

Rafe closed his eyes in frustration. "Fuck! I've already dealt with his ass once today!"

"It ain't over then. Morgan met Logan at her old apartment today, along with both of her parents. Callan gave Logan something to bind the demon's powers tonight. We have to make it happen."

Rafe took in a breath. "Meet me at ten at the station with Logan. Kai is coming with me. See you then." He put his phone down and rubbed above his eyebrows with his fingers. Maybe tonight would be the end of the demon, once and for all.

Destiny's soft voice broke through his thoughts. "More magick shit to deal with?"

Rafe raised his head and looked at her as he laughed. "You are what I need to keep me grounded, but...*magick shit?*" He laughed out loud. "I wouldn't tell Kinsley that's what you call her abilities!"

"And don't you dare repeat that, you ass!" she responded.

Rafe picked up his phone to text Kai. "I have to let him know Logan is coming and when I'm leaving. The two of you are staying here tonight?"

"I'd love it if Kinsley wanted to stay. It'd be an adult pajama party! I doubt we'll sleep until we hear back from you that you're all safe."

Rafe put his phone down. "They'll be here shortly, and the two of us have to leave."

Destiny reached for Rafe's hand. "Please be careful. I have no idea what you're up against out there, and yes, it scares me. I'll be here when you come back."

Kai and Kinsley knocked at the screen door and came in. Rafe watched them both for any signs of reconciliation. Neither of them seemed at odds with the other, but they weren't arm in arm either.

Destiny got up to hug her best friend, and brushed Kinsley's hair back to see her face. "Are you better?"

"I could ask the same? I think we're on the right path. I hope the two of you are. Tonight will be good for us to talk about shit we have never discussed. I hope you have an open mind!"

Destiny laughed. "I'm not sure. A lot has happened today. We'll get through it, and I will digest everything."

Rafe shook Kai's hand, hoping he took it as a sign of peace to forgive him for the attack. "Nate and Logan are meeting us. We need to go. Ladies, please do *not* roam the beach tonight. You're protected by wards here at the cabins. The beach is not." He reached out to hold Destiny, praying it wouldn't be the last time held her.

Kai stepped over to Kinsley and took her in his arms. Rafe was surprised at his reaction when he didn't feel anger toward Kai. That was a huge step, and he smiled for them.

Kinsley stepped away so they could leave. "Be safe guys. I know Logan will have your backs. Morgan is sending him for a reason. She knows what's coming that none of us know."

"Supposedly, her father has given Logan something that will bind the powers of Danteleon. Prayers would help." Rafe led the way out the door and Kai followed him to his car. Once they got in, he turned to Kai. "You sure you're up for more of what happened this afternoon?"

Kai nodded his head. "We got this! I don't know Logan, but I look forward to meeting him."

Rafe headed to the station. "Supposedly, he has more powers than any other witch in Pebble Cove, but he isn't even aware of all of his abilities."

Kai raised a brow. "It'll be an interesting night, and we'll be ready for anything."

Rafe and Kai walked into the station. Nate and Logan were in the conference room waiting with a fresh pot of coffee. As Rafe sat down across from Logan, he noticed Logan's hand on top of a black velvet bag. Whatever was inside, he hoped it contained their secret element for the success that they would need.

Logan appeared solemn, and Rafe did a double take, not remembering Logan to be as muscular as he looked tonight. Surely a few sessions at the gym with the weights could not have made that much of a difference in so little time. Then again, the boy was magickal...yet not so much a boy any longer.

"Logan, I'm glad we have you on our side tonight. I hear we may have our work cut out for us." Rafe enjoyed two swallows of his coffee.

"So I'm told. My grandfather said he'll join us once I contact him that we have this entity's powers bound...and he better not be late!"

Logan opened the black bag and carefully pulled out what Rafe would refer to as a medieval iron collar from a dungeon. The weight of it made Logan's forearms bulge as he held it. "I don't see a lock so how is that neck shackle going to hold him?"

"While we have him restrained long enough for me to get this around his neck, the minute these two ends meet, they seal themselves."

Logan passed it around for each of them to look at it and feel its weight.

Nate shook his head. "I wish the demon would have revealed exactly when and where we'll run into him. I should have brought Morgan's mirror."

Kai handed it back to Logan. "We're grateful that you're joining us tonight. We'll have each other's backs at all times."

"I can cloak our presence once we arrive. Jadis said that will confuse the demon and he can't track us so easily. I'm not sure of all of his powers, but then, I'm not sure of all of my *own* abilities. Perhaps I'll discover some of them tonight."

Nate proceeded to tell them the location Morgan saw in her mirror. "I know exactly where that is. If you look at the map we did over there on the war board, phone calls came in over a week ago at this location." Nate pointed to the Ravensville area. "Let's hope we can find this killer revisiting his scene of the crime."

Rafe glanced at Kai. "Do you have anything to add that we're missing?"

Kai looked at Logan, who didn't back down from the stare he got from Kai. "I've never dealt with magick and being invisible, so I'll play along with the plan. I do think we need to shift once we arrive. We'll be able to smell and sense the surroundings better."

"I agree." Rafe nodded.

Logan put the collar away. "I can cloak each one of you separate before you shift. If I do it as a group, I'm not sure how safe that would keep you. With my powers, we will all have telepathy to communicate."

Nate stood up. "Let's go. I think we're all more than ready to put an end to this killer."

Chapter 10

An hour later, Kai stood with the others in the dark, wooded area Nate had led them to. Kai wasn't new to working in the black darkness. Memories of his days as special forces in the remote jungles of Afghanistan sent a chill down his spin. Back then, he knew his men had his back. Tonight, he hoped it would be the same. His very life could be in just as much danger tonight, and he looked over his shoulder, smelling the damp earth and undergrowth of the forest. Not even a cricket chirped.

He paid close attention as Logan cloaked himself first, then began cloaking each one of them, and Kai took his turn. He then removed his boots, his shirt and jeans, while the others followed suit. Kai doubted that Logan had ever seen a shifter transform in front of him.

Logan watched closely. "Each of you can stay in touch via telepathy to keep your position known among us should you venture away from the group."

Before he shifted, Nate commented, "Morgan said she saw a body covered in leaves at the bottom of a deep ravine. I think that's where we need to go. Stay in touch as we search. Let's go!"

Kai shook out his hands and rolled his shoulders as his body began its transformation. He spread out his fingers as he ran, then leapt into the air, shifted to his cougar form, and landed on the dark road ahead. The others shifted and followed, with Logan close behind. He had impressed Kai and appeared to be comfortable taking charge and with their surroundings. Kai liked him.

Leading the group for several minutes, Kai caught a scent of decayed leaves off to his right. *Wait here a minute. I'll be right back!* he told the guys. In three leaps, Kai climbed a huge tree trunk to get a better view, his claws ripping at the bark for support as he climbed higher. With his keen feline night vision, he peered in all directions until he spotted a ravine. He took notice of the deep crevice's location and climbed down.

Before he got to the ground, he stopped as a ripple in the air caught his attention. He couldn't see anything, but he sure as hell felt the change. *Who else felt that?*

Rafe answered him. *We all did. Which way are we going?*

Kai leapt to the ground, the hair on his back standing on end. *There's a deep crevice half a mile west. Stay alert.*

Logan followed close. *The demon has arrived, guys. I'm glad you can sense him. Keep your wits about you.*

Crashing through the underbrush, Kai led the way toward the ravine. Whether it might be the right one, he couldn't say. His broad shoulders knocked smaller trees out of their way. He looked behind to make sure they followed and that nothing else followed them. The scent of the wet decayed leaves grew stronger.

Then another stench of foul, rotten eggs caught his sharp feline senses. A sure sign of a demon!

When he stopped, the others lined up at the edge of the ravine. The cloaking covered exactly where they stood, but the demon sensed that they were all there. In the silence, Kai's keen cougar eyesight pierced the darkness, searching for the source of the smell.

There, across the width of the ravine, on the other side, Kai caught sight of the gnarly teeth of a nine-foot creature, different from the one this afternoon, but massive just the same. He alerted the others to his find. *Everyone stand still. Let him make the first move. I know he can't see us, but he senses us the same as we sense him.*

Branches snapped and crunched when the creature swung his arms as he leapt down into the ravine. Landing half way down, he stood still, his head turning in both directions in search of his enemies.

Rafe bumped Kai's shoulder with his own and put his hand on Nate's shoulder. *Be ready. On three, we jump him at the same time! Logan, get ready!*

One!

Two!

Three!

Two wolves and a cougar landed halfway down the ravine, all leapt into the air toward the other side, and knocked the creature backward. Both of his arms tossed the wolves in the air, and Kai hugged his torso with four cougar paws, hoping the wolves would return to help. Before they could arrive, the cougar chewed into a shoulder and the creature yowled. The wolves returned and each bit into a leg. A yelp rang out as the creature bent to grab a wolf around its neck, and he flung it into the darkness. The other wolf pounced onto the cougar's back to add his weight, knocking the creature backward onto the ground.

It rolled twice, leaving Kai on top, and he hung on tight, his claws digging deeper into the creature's back as it howled. Then Kai felt huge claws around his ribs, pulling him away. He swiped at the creature's mouth and face before he went flying through the air.

The tree trunk that Kai hit knocked the wind from his lungs for a moment before he landed at the bottom. He shook his head to regain his bearings and ran back into the fray of flying limbs. One lone wolf had jumped at the creature's chest, and knocked him to the ground yet again, but it rolled over and stood up, ready for more.

Darkness still shrouded the ravine, and only faint shadows could be seen until Logan held up a light for Kai to see enough to make it back to save the wolf. He worried where the other wolf lay but helping the one in trouble came first.

Kai snuck around behind the creature, and with full force, knocked it forward to land face down as Kai landed four huge paws on its back while it lay flattened. *Logan, hurry! We might not get another chance.*

As a wolf bit into a flailing arm, Kai caught the glint of steel around the creature's throat and heard metal snap together. Beneath Kai's paws, the creature shifted into human form, making the smell of evil even worse, but Kai stayed on its back. *Logan, what now? We didn't bring a rope.*

Not a problem. I've got this. Jump away!

Logan pointed at the dark warlock. His body lifted and went vertically in the air. With Kai's keen eyesight, he watched a rope wrap around the length of the suspended body, then dropped him in a heap on the ground. The man was at least his own height and weight, with dark curly hair.

Logan touched his ring and twisted it. *Grandfather, I need you now! We've got him! He's all yours!*

Kai shifted and saw Rafe shift. He looked around, in all directions. *Where's Nate?*

Logan held out a lantern to Kai. *Use this to find him. I'm waiting for my grandfather, then I'll catch up to you.*

Taking the lantern, he and Rafe went in search of Nate, but the thick underbrush and darkness hindered them. The steepness of the ravine wall made walking harder. *If he was thrown over here, he could have easily rolled to the bottom.*

Rafe called out for Nate, and they listened.

Twigs snapped further down in the ravine and a wolf howled.

Why hasn't he shifted back yet? Kai dodged small trees on his way down behind Rafe, and he saw a wolf, the fur covered in blood, laying on his side. Rafe got to Nate first.

When Kai approached, the light allowed him to see the bloody gash torn into the tender area beneath his ribcage and one leg at a weird angle.

"Don't move him yet, in case his back is broken. Nate, can you move your paws at all?"

Both front paws wiggled.

"Good sign. You've got another gash on your left shoulder. Just stay still." Kai moved his fingers gently over the shoulder bones, checking for anything that might be broken. "Can you shift back?"

I don't think so, but...take that light down to the bottom and look around. I smell death down there.

"Don't move, Logan will be here shortly. We'll be right back." Kai grabbed the lantern, nodded at Rafe, and led the way to the bottom. His feet got wet as the smell led them closer. Kai stepped on something and held out his arm to halt Rafe.

As Kai lifted the lantern, a tennis shoe peeked out from beneath the wet leaves. He looked at Rafe.

"Shit. I know it's late, but once we get Nate fixed, I'll call the coroner. Nate comes first. Come on." Rafe went back up the hill where Nate lay, and he'd been able to shift back.

Kai knelt at Nate's broken leg and set the lantern down so he could use both hands on the leg. "Easy, buddy." Carefully, he moved his fingers up the bones from the ankle, the sticky blood coating his own fingers. The tibia was broken there. He felt above the knee and found a break in the femur. "Shit!"

Rafe moved closer. "How bad is it?"

"His bones above and below the knee are busted. We can't move him. I'm guessing his shoulder is out, too, but I didn't feel any broken bones up there."

My grandfather has taken Danteleon away. Where are you guys? Swing your light so I can see.

Kai stood, raised the lantern, and gently swung it for Logan. In an instant, he appeared at their side. "Damn, dude!"

"Sorry. I'm still getting used to this, too. Nate isn't in good shape, is he?" Logan knelt beside Nate, his hands hovering over the length of his leg.

Kai held the light closer to watch Logan spread out his long fingers over Nate's lower leg above the broken bone. He heard Logan mumble a few words. Again, magick happened before his eyes as the leg slowly moved into place while Logan rubbed his fingers over the area.

Nate screamed out in pain.

Kai watched the bloody gash close but not heal all the way. Logan moved his hands over Nate's thigh and that wound closed. He rubbed over the muscular thigh as though he massaged it, making Nate scream out again, then abruptly stop. Kai assumed he'd passed out but couldn't take his eyes away from Logan's healing fingers and the magick he'd never witnessed.

Never had he seen anyone heal with their hands. Nate's thigh slowly moved until it was straight. "His shoulder is banged up while you're at it!"

Logan gave him a smile. "Thanks for letting me know. He might not be able to walk well for a while. It's gotta heal, but I can teleport us up to the car." He moved his hands over Nate's shoulder, massaged a bit and stopped. "Nate, can you hear me. You have to wake up or my mom's gonna kick my ass." Logan gently shook Nate.

Nate squeezed his eyes tight before he opened them.

"Welcome, back. Mom will be happy, and I get to live another day. We need to stand you up. I think I fixed your leg, for the most part. It's going to be sore so stand on your right leg once we get you up."

Kai and Rafe got Nate on his feet, and he put his right arm over Rafe's shoulder.

Logan put his palm out in front of Kai and Rafe. "We all need to join hands. I'll teleport us to the car."

Rafe's hand covered Logan's. "Once we're up there, I need to call the coroner. There's a body down there under the leaves. We'll come back down for it."

Kai joined hands with the others and every nerve in his body tingled. In the blink of an eye, they all stood outside the patrol car.

As Logan waved his hand in front of Nate, his clothing appeared on his body. "I figured you were too sore to try and dress yourself. I hope your jeans got on right."

Nate checked the zipper and button, then laughed. "Thanks, man."

Kai tossed Rafe his clothes and the two got dressed.

"Logan, can you put Nate in the backseat so he's comfortable? You don't need to be here when the coroner shows up. He'll ask too many questions."

"Sure thing, sir." Logan looked at Nate. "Let's get you comfortable, then I need to go see Mandy. I'll meet you at your house later."

Rafe carefully put his hand on Nate's good shoulder. "Get some rest. When the coroner is gone, we'll get you home."

Kai straightened his tee shirt as he watched the guys, and hoped Nate would heal okay. He leaned into the back door of the car to talk to Nate. "You had some nasty broken bones, dude. Take it easy."

In a flash, Logan disappeared, and Kai shook his head. "I'll never get used to that! That's crazy shit, right there." It made him think about how his world would change now that Kinsley would be a part of it. Something to look forward to, for sure.

"It does take some getting used to when they disappear in front of you. Welcome to *our* world!" Rafe dug around in the car for his phone. "I hate to get anyone up at this hour of the night, but the coroner needs to retrieve the body."

Rafe gave someone the directions out here and advised them to bring the fire department so the body could be hoisted up from the ravine.

Thirty minutes later, the fire department arrived with the coroner, and Kai watched them drag the ropes and gurney down the hill. Rafe talked with the coroner as Kai took mental notes on all involved. The coroner looked like death warmed over at this late hour. He didn't seem at all surprised that a body would end up clear out here, deep in a ravine and Kai found that a bit odd. Prior knowledge? The coroner didn't ask many questions, but said he'd be in touch in the morning.

Kai and Rafe stuck around until the last firefighter left the scene, and he and Rafe got in the car. "Nate, you still hanging in there? We'll have you home shortly."

Kai pulled out his phone. "I'll call Kinsley while you drive. They should be at Morgan's when we arrive."

* * * * *

Kinsley paced Destiny's kitchen after the guys left. She worried about all three men and what they might run into. They could easily come across the killer and then anything could go wrong. At least Logan was going to be with them, but that still confused her. Why would Logan need to be at the investigation?

She heard the screen door rattle, and it jarred her, but she knew the wards protected them and they weren't expecting anyone. When she peeked out the screen, she didn't see anything, and the hair on her neck stood up.

"Are you going to open the door so I can come in or are you just going to leave me out here all night?"

"Gibbs? What the hell?"

Gibbs stood on his hind legs, tapping a toe. "Angela's garden was all the buzz tonight with some sort of a disturbance in the air. They told me I better get to the cabins."

When Kinsley opened the door, he scurried inside. Destiny screamed and grabbed the broom, taking swings at Gibbs while he ran circles around Kinsley's legs.

Destiny's wide-eyed gaze looked hilarious. "Stand still and I can get him out of here!"

Kinsley took the broom from Destiny. "Hon...he's my pet. It's okay!"

Her eyes couldn't get any wider as she threw up her hands. "And since when do rodents talk? This day has totally gone to shit!"

"Des, let's get comfy on the couch. I'll explain. Come on. I know you have a ton of questions for me."

"You've got that right!"

Kinsley filled her glass with ice and water. She needed to dilute all the whiskey she'd drank, then went to sit on the couch with Destiny. When she sat down, Gibbs climbed up at her side furthest away from Destiny. "I can't imagine the shit going on in your head right now. Mortals think magick is just fantasy, not something real. We have to be very careful around them."

"Your secret is safe with me. I promise. I think." Destiny shook her head as she peeked around Kinsley to look at Gibbs. "I thought the most shocking was to see the guys shift into a wolf and cougar right in front of me, but he's got that beat. Talking pets? Now I've heard it all!"

Kinsley patted her lap, and Gibbs cautiously climbed over. She ran her hand over his back. "She wouldn't hurt a flea, hon."

Gibbs quickly looked up at her. "I think you're nuts if you believe that. The way she handles a broom, she must be a witch, too."

That was a good starting spot for Kinsley. "Most witches have a familiar around them who help. Gibbs can talk to the trees and plants in Angela's garden. They keep each other aware of what's going on, and then they tell us."

Destiny rolled her eyes and stared at the ceiling. "Just wake me up when this is over."

Kinsley scratched Gibbs under his chin. "She's had a trying day today after witnessing magick, demons, and shifting. It might take her a while to understand it all."

"Back to the shifting shit. How do you know when they're going to shift? Do they give you a warning? Oh my gosh..." Destiny peered around the room as though someone might hear them. "Does sex make them shift? That'd be too weird. I'm not really into that, Kins!"

Gibbs nudged Kinsley's hand. "Is she for real?"

Destiny's comments made Kinsley and Gibbs both laugh. "Now that I think about it, Rafe has had his claws come out when he got turned on."

Her eyes got huge, and she leaned closer. "He's scratched you?"

"Not a scratch, more like a poke. He just had to breathe and get control of himself, and his claws go back in."

Gibbs popped his head up. "I told you before, if you had more sex with him, he wouldn't lose control like that!"

"Gibbs! Stop!" Kinsley used her fingers to shut Gibbs mouth but looked at Destiny. "Are you in the least interested in Rafe? I think he's really got a thing for you."

Destiny put a hand up. "I'm not one to step into love triangles. You two have a thing, and I thought it was pretty serious."

"He's a sweetheart, hon. Our problem was me. My heart was always hoping for Kai to return, somehow. It sounds silly now. We haven't had contact in twenty-five years, and suddenly he shows up out of the blue?"

Kinsley stretched her legs out, rested her feet on the small ottoman, and Gibbs curled up on her lap. "I was fuming mad last week when we saw each other at the Dragon's Lair down in Hag Stone. Angry that he hadn't bothered to call me in twenty-five years, angry back then that he left without saying a word. I know I went off to college, but he still knew my phone number. I've let the anger toward him build all these years. When I saw him, it blew up that day, and I've been pissed since then. And not knowing where he was or if I'd ever see him again!"

"Did you know *his* phone number?"

Kinsley stared at her like she had two heads. "If he was still interested, he would have called *me.*"

Her friend held up a hand to ward off any backlash. "I was just asking!"

Kinsley toyed with her water and ice. "Sorry, I know." She looked up and met Destiny's gaze. "When he stormed out onto the back porch tonight and kissed me, I was shocked to my toes. I had no idea he still had feelings that might match mine. But my goddess, his kiss let me know if his words didn't. Damn, I forgot just how good he was!" She touched her lips where his had bruised hers, and her toes curled just thinking about their next encounter. "How far will he go next time we're alone?"

Gibbs had to put in his two cents. "I'll be around to make sure he doesn't go too far!"

Destiny cleared her throat. "How far will you *let* him go next time? Did you two have sex in high school? Never mind, that's none of my business."

Kinsley looked away and didn't answer right away, wishing they *would* have had sex back then. "No, we never went that far."

Destiny leaned forward. "Could you stop him? Would you *want* to? I'm not sure I could if I were you. He's sexy as hell, and I'm not sure he realizes just how sexy he is. But that's a good thing in a man."

Gibbs scratched his ear. "I'm pretty sexy!"

"Yes, you are, little man! He's got several girlfriends, I think." Kinsley picked him and kissed his nose, then put Gibbs back on her lap. "All these years, I've done nothing but think about the day we'd come face to face again. Today sure as hell wasn't even close to how I'd imagined it would be. I was shocked to see Rafe attack Kai like that though. I hope the cuts they gave each other heal okay."

"Rafe's were pretty deep, but cougar claws are longer, I think. He better be careful claiming you! If I see one scratch on your skin..."

Gibbs chimed in again. "I'll be around to make sure he doesn't get out of line with her."

"You two! I don't think it'll be like that, but I *have* thought of what it would be like with Kai." Images swam through Kinsley's mind. She couldn't deny she wanted him but remembered how pissed she was in the bar the day she saw him. *Why can't I stay mad and stand my ground?* All these years, she'd been angry that he never called her when, in fact, she could have called him just as easily.

His touch sent shivers over her skin, and his kisses tore at her senses. A man that passionate could mess with a woman's mind. She couldn't think straight when Kai was around and imagining him naked made her heart race. He could look at her and strip her naked. The real thing would be hot and heavy, for sure.

Destiny tapped her thigh and handed her a small plate of sliced beef stick and cheese with crackers. "You were in your own little world there for a while, so I cut some munchies up for us. Gibbs even helped!"

Kinsley looked up at her best friend. "I didn't realize you even got up to go in the kitchen. I'm sorry. Thanks for this."

"You have it bad, girl! Just so you know. How have you made it through the last twenty-five years without him in your life? You can't keep your heart closed forever. I wish you would have called me more often and we had talked about him."

"I didn't realize it either. It's been hours since the guys left. I'm getting worried."

Destiny grabbed her phone. "It's nearly four am!"

"No way!" Kinsley finished her snack and set her plate aside. When her phone rang, Kai's face appeared. She stared at Destiny and answered immediately. "Hey!"

"We're on our way back. I need you to meet us at Morgan's. Call her, let her know we're on our way. I'll see you at her place. Please teleport.

I'll explain when I see you. Sorry, I don't mean to give orders, but we need you."

"Sure, sure. I'll call her now." Her line went dead, and she stared at Destiny, then dialed Morgan's number.

Chapter 11

Morgan put her phone down after Kinsley hung up, and she paced the kitchen waiting for her to arrive. She had no idea why Rafe and Kai would want Kinsley here when the guys got back, and it was four-thirty in the morning. *What the hell?* She rubbed her arms the same time Kinsley popped into her kitchen with Destiny.

Destiny put her arms out to steady herself as they appeared. "Holy shit, Kins! What the hell did we just do? That sent shock waves through my whole body!"

Kinsley put an arm around her friend. "That's what magick feels like, but we made it."

Destiny shook out her arms and fingers as she looked from Morgan to Kinsley with wide eyes. "Will I ever understand all this magick shit?"

Kinsley laughed. "Not at the moment, hon. But I need you to be with us, and not alone at the cabin."

Morgan had already guessed that Destiny was a mortal the last time she'd visited. "I'll pour some wine. She looks like she needs it. Des, you better take a seat at the island."

Morgan passed out the glasses and took a sip. "Do you have any idea what's going on with the guys?" She feared one of them must be hurt or everyone wouldn't be gathering at her place. When the demon's vision appeared in her mirror, she knew this mission in Ravensville wouldn't be a walk in the park.

"I don't. Kai just said to meet them here." Kinsley sat at the island with Morgan and Destiny.

The three of them talked of the dangers they could have faced with *Danteleon* stalking them while they searched for a body. Morgan twisted the stem of her wine glass. "I can't help but think this is my fault because he's after *me*, not everyone else, due to this insane family promise centuries ago!" Morgan watched the other two women closely. Something had changed about each of them, she just couldn't put her finger on it. "Both of you seem different today.

Something's happened. You have a calm aura around you. What are you not telling me?"

Kinsley stared into her wine like the answer was floating there. "It's been a busy twenty-four hours, hon." She met Morgan's gaze. "When all of this has calmed down, we can talk about it, but *he* was at the cabins this afternoon."

She was relieved that Kinsley hadn't said *his* name out loud again, but the danger he presented would never let up until her father had him captured and back to the Council's prison.

Fifteen minutes later, Morgan saw the flashing lights on the patrol car as it turned into the driveway. She ran out to the porch and met them before the guys even got out. She saw Rafe and Kai, but not Nate, and her heart sank. Where was Nate and why wasn't he out of the car?

Kinsley put her arm around Morgan's waist. "Don't jump to conclusions, hon."

Kai looked directly at Kinsley as he got out of the car. "We'll need some towels, babe. Hurry. Both of you go inside. We'll be right there."

Morgan refused to budge.

Kai fisted his hands. "Take her inside! Now!"

Kinsley tugged on Morgan's arm until she moved. Morgan wanted to know what happened to Nate and why they wouldn't let her be out there with him.

Against her will, she let Kinsley drag her inside. "Where are your bath towels? Can you get several? I have no idea why they want them."

Morgan hurried to the linen closet and pulled out four bath towels. As she turned back toward the kitchen, Rafe and Kai were carrying Nate inside. Blood covered his clothes; his face, arms, and chest were clawed to pieces.

She grabbed the island counter for support and dropped the towels.

Was he dead?

He certainly looked like it, and her knees weakened. She couldn't lose Nate!

Kinsley picked up the towels, ran toward the sofa, and laid down two towels, then stepped back so the guys could place Nate on the couch. "I'll get some water and bandages."

Morgan ran to Nate's side and knelt, taking his hand in hers. She pressed her fingers to his wrist and held her breath until she felt a pulse.

Kinsley handed her a warm cloth and she wiped Nate's eyes, careful not to reopen any wounds. He didn't move while she gently dabbed at his face. "What happened, guys?"

Rafe exchanged glances with Kinsley. "Danteleon met us in the woods. He threw Nate in the air and slammed him against a tree. Nate was fierce, but you can't fight the evil we ran into tonight. Our pack members stick together, and no one gets left behind. Thank God Logan was with us. I've never seen that kind of power, Morgan. Logan healed Nate's broken left leg in two places and put his shoulder back in the socket. I wasn't aware Logan was a healer."

Morgan gasped when she met Rafe's eyes. "Is Logan okay?" *Goddess let him be alive!* Rafe had paused too long for her comfort. "Tell me the truth! If he's not, I'll kill Danteleon myself!" Her fingers fisted around the cloth she held up.

Rafe nodded, and her heart continued beating. "He had to check in with Mandy, but he'll be here soon."

She would die if her son would have been killed by him. Morgan took another warm cloth from Kinsley and dabbed at the cuts on Nate's face and neck. Tears pooled and blurred her vision, not sure what she'd do if she lost Nate.

When he turned his head toward her, he opened his eyes as he reached for her face. His bloody thumb wiped the tears from her cheek. "I'm good, baby." His crooked smile didn't make her feel better, but at least he was talking.

"I love you. Don't you dare give up tonight. We'll get you fixed." Her hand shook so badly she could barely hold the cloth. Kinsley wiped Nate's feet to help get the blood cleaned up. The two of them worked together, but Morgan had never seen such violence that could cause this kind of damage. She tried not to cry as they rinsed the bloody cloths and started over.

"Mom..."

Morgan's breath caught in her throat as she looked up to see her son. She couldn't stop the tears when she saw him as he stood in the doorway of the living room.

"I did my best to protect him, Mom. Honest."

Morgan covered her mouth to stop a sob.

Logan set aside his backpack. He knelt beside Morgan and hugged her tight. Her heart swelled with so much love, knowing that Logan would care for Nate when he was injured.

He brushed her hair from her face. "He'll be okay. His left leg was in bad shape. As soon as I put both hands on his broken femur...Mom, the bones moved beneath my fingers, and I felt them straighten back into place. I didn't move them! It shocked me, but I knew I had to heal his tibia, too. If you'll let me, I want to see if I can heal his wounds." Logan waited for her reply before he moved.

She reached up to touch Logan's cheek. Through her tears she could see his concern, and she scooted back to give Logan room. "Please help his pain."

Logan knelt beside Nate while Morgan held his hand. Nate had closed his eyes again but held tight to her hand. First Logan placed his palms on Nate's cheeks and his fingertips on his temples. As Morgan watched, Nate's deepest cuts moved slightly as the skin came together and sealed. The cut still appeared raw, but not bleeding. His swollen lips reduced back to normal.

With magick, Logan peeled away Nate's tee shirt, revealing badly bruised ribs and torn flesh. Logan hovered his hands over the rib area and when he touched the skin, the bones visibly moved under Logan's fingers and the bruising lightened. Nate moved his head as he groaned, but didn't open his eyes. More of his cuts closed up.

Morgan prayed silently when she glanced over at Kinsley as they watched her son work his magick. "My mother is a healer, too. It's a special ability. I'm glad Logan inherited that."

"I can't wait to face *him* again. I'll incinerate him on the spot like I should have done the first time I saw him! I won't allow him to rule my life with threats of stealing me away. I'll finish it!" Morgan envisioned the demon burning at her hand and cherished the end result, wishing it were true.

With his special abilities, Logan cut the jeans with his fingers to heal the deep wounds that still remained on Nate's thighs. "You won't have to worry about *him*, mom. With the help of Rafe and Kai, we got the shackle around his neck. He's powerless now. Grandpa showed up out there and took him to face the Witch's Council and their jail."

"Oh my goddess! Is that true?"

Logan looked at her with raised brows, then turned his attention back to Nate. An hour later, Logan sat on the floor next to Morgan, exhausted from the ordeal of healing. She placed a hand on his thigh. "Thank you, son."

Kinsley sat beside Logan and hugged him. When she snapped her fingers, three mugs of steaming herbal tea appeared in her hand. She handed one to Rafe, Kai, and Logan. "You've all been through a rough night. Drink this potion to restore your strength. Healing others isn't something to be taken lightly, Logan. Your grandmother passed out after healing Nate on the beach when *he* tried to kill Nate that time. Don't over-tax your system for twenty-four hours."

Morgan watched as Logan sipped the tea, thankful Kinsley had come to help them get through the night. After several sips, Morgan saw Logan's color change from pasty white to a healthy pink. "You need to rest, hon."

"I have to get back to Mandy. She knew it would be a long night. I promised I would return when this was over. Nate will sleep for a while. I pushed some of my strength through to him. He's going to be sore for a few days as he continues to heal, and the scars will disappear. You won't know he was even attacked." Logan handed the mug back to Kinsley. "Thank you for that. I already feel stronger, but I'm learning my limits."

He stood up, grabbed his backpack, then bent down to kiss Morgan's cheek. "You might want to teleport him to your bedroom where he can rest better. I'll call tomorrow to see how he's doing. I love you, mom."

She watched her son leave, proud of the man he was becoming. The weight that his shoulders would carry into his future would make him even stronger. Morgan turned her attention back to Nate. She rinsed a cloth in the water and washed the back of Nate's hands, praying to the goddess that he'd be okay and hopefully not remember much of the night's events.

Nate's features looked rugged. He must have fought hard against the demon in her honor.

She lightly stroked his cheek, brushed the hair from his forehead, and placed his hand on his stomach so he could rest. Morgan took in a deep breath, glad that her son was able to heal the love of her life and her new reason to be alive.

When she searched the faces of the men who had saved her mate, she saw so much love, but Rafe sat next to Destiny, their fingers laced together, and Kai had his arm around Kinsley as she leaned against his shoulder. Kinsley gave her a wink and a one-sided smile.

"That's what has changed. I felt it, you know. I can't wait to hear *this* story! Let's sit in the kitchen so Nate can rest. I think we all need a stiff drink."

Morgan sat the bottle of whiskey on the counter but filled her glass with wine; the day had definitely been a long one. She knew the universe still had more news for her once her friends told their stories.

She listened intently as the guys retold their stories of the attack at the beach and the attack in the woods. Best of all they told her how strong her son had been throughout the ordeal and how her father had come through to remove the danger from all of their lives.

Morgan circled her finger toward the four of them. "This sudden change had to come as a surprise to all of you, but from the looks on your faces, and the vibe I'm receiving, it appears all has a happy ending?"

Kai swirled the ice in his glass and glanced at Kinsley. "I think we all have some issues to work out, but for the most part, we've all come to an agreement."

Kinsley reached out to cover his forearm with her fingers. "We have. The results won't happen overnight, but yes, we're on the right track."

Morgan couldn't deny Kai's good looks. His shoulders were wider than Nate's, and his chest looked rock hard, not to mention the muscles in his forearms. She squirmed on her chair.

Destiny bumped her shoulder into Kinsley. "I kind of feel left out in all of this since I don't have any magick in my bones. And I've yet to understand this world you all live in, so give me a break until I catch up. These demons sound horrible to deal with. I'm glad Logan was able to use his powers tonight."

"I think we should get out of your way so you and Nate can rest. Not to mention the four of us need some rest." Rafe leaned toward Kinsley. "We do need your magick touch in the back of my patrol car. It's a bit bloody and I doubt you two want to sit back there until you can do your thing to clean it up."

Kinsley smiled. "I'd be happy to. Let's head out of here. Hon, keep us posted on Nate's recovery." She gave Morgan a hug.

She held onto Kinsley for a moment, so thankful she had friends in Pebble Cove who cared for her and Nate. "Thank you again, guys." Morgan kissed Kinsley's cheek. "Be happy. You all deserve it."

"We will. Take care of him."

* * * * *

Kai held hands with Kinsley as they made their way in the dark over to his cabin, the porch light guiding their way. He unlocked the door, picked Kinsley up in his arms and used her feet to push the door open. He loved the feel of her arms around his neck.

"Carrying me over the threshold. Is there something I need to know ahead of time?"

He pushed the door shut behind them and listened for it to lock. Then he let her legs drop and pulled her close. "I'm afraid if I let go of you, you'll disappear, and I'll never find you again." His knuckle lightly caressed the soft curve of her cheek. Her eyes bore the signs of exhaustion. "Is it bad that I just want to hold you forever?"

When her warm hand smoothed over his chest, every nerve in his body woke up. As their gazes held, her nails lightly caressed a trail down the side of his neck. In doing so, he couldn't resist her any longer and kissed her with a hunger he hadn't felt for a woman before. He fisted his fingers into the back of her hair, holding her to him.

She molded her body to his like they were meant for each other. He memorized the curves of her back, her waist and her ass, that fit perfectly into his hand. When he lifted her, her legs wrapped around his hips. Their kiss seemed to last an eternity as they devoured each other at the door.

He pulled from the kiss, touched his lips to hers once, then pressed his forehead to hers. "I need you, but I need a shower first."

"Let me down. I'm sorry I didn't check your wounds first. See what you do in my head! Let me see how bad your cuts are." She wiggled from his arms and turned them as she assessed the damages. As he watched, the dirt and dried blood disappeared and so did some of his pain. "I'm not a healer like my mother or Logan, but I can clean these up. When she finished, she grabbed the bottom of his tee shirt and lifted it.

"Are you going to have your way with me right here before I shower? Because I can make that happen for you."

She stomped her foot, and he laughed at her, but bent enough so she could pull his shirt over his head. Her eyes roamed his chest, and then her hands were all over him. The sensations made him dizzy after only dreaming about her, and now, to have her this close was overwhelming. He rolled his shoulders to relieve some of the tension from the ordeal tonight.

"I love the feel of your muscles rippling beneath my fingers, but you have to relax. I want to remove some of the knots and pain in your muscles."

"There is only one way to remove the tight knot I have in a muscle that truly hurts, babe. Your fingers are like magick, and I can think of a better use for them."

Her nails dug into his skin, and he yelped at her. "That's not helping." As she smoothed over his chest, the tension went away. Her hands moved down his sides and he winced.

"Sorry, hon. These deep cuts are from his claws. I hope they don't get infected. I can't close them, but we might have to have Logan check these. I hate that all of you got hurt so badly getting *him* under control. Thank you for what you did for Nate. Morgan will never forget it."

"Like Rafe said, pack members never leave anyone behind!"

Kinsley turned him to face the door, then again, her hands moved lightly over his back and shoulders. "These are cleaning up nicely. I just wish I could heal and close them up. A shower will clean them out for sure, but a few of these I'll have to use ointment on. Angela has some stuff that fixes everything."

"Angela?"

"My roommate at home." Kinsley laughed. "Yes, she's a witch, too."

How much more did he need to learn about Kinsley? They'd been apart for so long; it was like meeting for the first time. *One day at a time.* They would get through it.

Warm lips touched his back and hands moved around his waist and up his stomach as she hugged him. "Goddess, your body is beautiful. I love touching you."

"If you aren't careful, I'll be shifting right here, and it won't be pretty."

"Then I guess you better learn how to control that, detective."

He turned in her arms, cupped her face, and searched her eyes. Kai considered himself the lucky one to be able to have a mate so tender and thoughtful. He couldn't believe he'd never mated with her when they were in high school. Then again, he had no idea he was a shifter back then. Fate had put them together, but didn't make them realize they needed one another.

So many things went wrong for them. He didn't understand why fate had dealt them a bad hand, but rediscovering each was going to be heaven. Her eyes watched him. They were deep green pools, and he wanted to see deeper. "You are so complex, but I'm glad you're finally mine again." When he kissed her, their lips melted into one another and her tongue teased him to no end.

Kai pulled from their kiss and breathed in deep. "We're taking a shower. You can get your clothes wet or remove them. I don't care either way." He saw the indecisive thoughts swirling in her mind and knew what they were. "No, I haven't seen you naked in twenty-five years, but one way or another, I will...tonight."

"But...are we ready for that step?"

"Seeing you naked or taking you as my mate? They aren't the same thing."

Her cheeks flushed bright pink, and he scooped her close. Her nearness overwhelmed his senses. He didn't remember this happening as bad when they were younger, but now...he knew what it was like to make love to a woman. Imagining Kinsley beneath him made him crazy with need and he wouldn't give up on making her his mate. "I want you, babe, there is no doubt about that, but when I mate as a shifter, it will be because we are *both* ready. That won't be tonight. I don't have the energy. I do want to hold you while I sleep and know you're safe."

"Well...I don't want to get my clothes wet."

Kai gently squeezed her ass and reluctantly released her from his embrace. "Lead the way, woman." He watched her slender hips sway as she walked toward the bathroom and his heart was finally happy. She'd pulled her shirt over her head and swirled it in the air before letting it drop in the hall.

Chapter 12

Once everyone had gone home for the night, or rather morning, Morgan quietly walked in to check on Nate. His chest rose with each breath, and she relaxed, knowing he still lived. She went to their room, turned down his side of the bed, and fluffed his pillow before bringing him in.

Back in the living room, she took his hand in hers, thought about his side of the bed, and hoped she didn't wake him during the teleport. At least magick was good for something, otherwise she would not have been able to get Nate to bed on her own.

The tingle of magick surged through her body as she teleported to their bedroom. She made sure Nate's head lay centered on the pillow, then pulled the covers over him. Realizing how exhausted she was, Morgan readied for bed, then climbed in beside Nate. Cuddling would be out of the question since she didn't want to cause him more pain. When he moved his hand beneath the covers in search of her hand, she took it. His fingers squeezed her once and then he slept peacefully.

She tried not to think of how close she came to not having him with her tonight. The goddess was on their side...and at Logan's side when he healed Nate. She took a thankful deep breath, got in a comfortable position still holding Nate's hand, and dozed into dreams of her and Nate.

Before he opened his eyes, Nate realized pain like he hadn't felt in years. He tried to remember the events of the night before and couldn't. *How can that be? I know we went to Ravensville!* Mentally, he assessed his injuries, slowly scrunched his shoulders as a stabbing pain went through the muscles. When he moved his left foot to the side, a pain shot straight up his leg, making him gasp.

Nate knew he was in his own bed and slowly turned his head toward Morgan. She slept peacefully, hair partially covering her face. Very slowly, he turned onto his right side, realizing too late how painful that was. He yelped a bit too loud, and Morgan opened her eyes and raised up on her elbow.

Nate cringed. "Sorry, babe. I didn't mean to wake you. I didn't realize turning over would hurt so much. What the hell happened?"

"You were badly injured when Rafe and Kai brought you home last night. Logan healed you the best he could, like my mom does. It must have worked. The cuts on your face have nearly disappeared." She pulled the sheet back to see his chest. "Your wounds are healed. Logan said it might take a few days for them to disappear." Morgan caressed his cheek and threaded back the hair on his forehead as she searched his eyes. "Don't you remember anything?"

"I've tried. Last night is a blank. Why?" He struggled with not remembering.

"I'll have to check with Logan later today. He may have been able to wipe the memory from your mind. You don't want to remember last night. Your left leg was broken in two places, you had very deep claw cuts on your sides, chest and back, and your shoulder was out of place. He healed you and I can't thank him enough for saving you. If you would have bled out, I don't know what I would have done."

"I remember driving there with Rafe and Kai and knowing we had to deal with Danteleon. That's it. There's no recollection of even seeing him."

"Then let's not worry about it today. You guys were able to detain him long enough for Logan to shackle him for my father. He won't be a problem anymore. I want you to heal and rest. Logan said you'll need a few days for your bones to grow back where the breaks were." She kissed him tenderly and the warmth of her lips relaxed him.

"Logan better be able to fill in all of the details when we see him. I want to know what went down. For now, I need some strong coffee and aspirins." Shit! He'd have to roll back the other way and sit up for that.

Morgan presented him with a straw in a glass of water, and three white pills. "Let's start with these.

He smiled as he looked at her. "You and your magick do come in handy at times. Is a coffee that easy, too?"

She sat up and held out her palm. A large mug of steaming liquid appeared. Morgan blew across the top of the coffee, and he immediately smelled the strong brew.

"I love you!" He swallowed the aspirins with the water and switched drinks with her.

"I think we can make you comfortable in here this morning and not have to make you move yet." She waved her hand, and four pillows appeared behind him, and she helped him prop up sideways on the others. "Is that better?"

He laughed but inside, he wanted to scream from the pain of moving, yet refused to let her see it. Hopefully, time and rest would work to his advantage.

"I'll get your cell phone in a bit. I'm sure Rafe is still catching up on sleep, too. They all left about five this morning. You let me know when you're hungry. I'll see what I can conjure up for us!" With a wink, she got herself comfortable next to him.

* * * * *

Rafe had dragged Kai out of bed after the coroner called him this morning. He wanted Kai with him when they talked with the coroner at the morgue, and Kai followed him inside, where they were led to the exam room. The body of the victim had already been washed by Dr. Grissom and the woman with him looked up at Rafe for a second and went back to writing down notes as she examined the body.

"Rafe, I'm glad you were able to come down. This is my assistant, Dr. Lydia Rigor. I don't think you've met her before." Grissom wiped his hands on a towel.

"A pleasure to meet you, Doctor." She didn't look up but raised her pen and kept working. He couldn't ignore that fact and wondered what she was hiding. "Have you found any evidence that we can use to catch this asshole? That's my main goal, and so far, we've found nothing at any of the locations." Rafe glanced at Kai, but his attention was on Dr. Rigor. The woman ignored both of them, and he'd get Kai's take on her disinterest when they got back to the car.

"I've gone over each body we've found, and nothing has been pulled from any of the victims. The organ removal in all the victims is too exact to be your average murderer. Whoever our perp is, they're covering their tracks too well. I've not found carpet fibers, no unknown hair strands, no epithelial cells from a different donor, but..."

Dr. Grissom paused as if he were thinking how to phrase something, and Rafe stepped closer. "I did pull a few samples of lung tissue and found mold spores. It makes me wonder if this victim wasn't held somewhere before they were killed."

A clipboard crashed to the floor that Dr. Rigor had been taking notes on, and she rushed to pick it up. "Sorry, Doctor. I didn't mean to be so clumsy and interrupt your conversation."

After Rafe noted her hoarse voice, he saw Kai pick up her clipboard, then hand it to her. He didn't let go of the clipboard until she made eye-contact with him and then turned back to the victim's body. Dr. Rigor began coughing for several moments, and the guys stopped talking. When she recovered, she apologized and went back to work on her notes.

Again, not making longer eye contact was odd behavior for anyone. And Rafe made a mental note of her coughing and hoarseness.

The hairs on the back of Rafe's neck stood up. "So maybe we need to investigate any old cabins in the area that look a bit run down and not occupied. I have a few in mind that I know of, and we'll look for others. Thanks for talking to us today, Grissom. Let me know if you find anything else."

Rafe turned to leave but paused. "Dr. Rigor, have you worked with Dr. Grissom here in the morgue very long? I don't remember seeing you before."

Her pen fell onto the table next to the body and she quickly picked it up. "I've been here for about six months." The woman rearranged the papers on her clipboard and began making new notes but wouldn't look at Rafe.

"Good. Keep Grissom in line for me." Rafe glanced at Grissom. "Talk to you later."

He and Kai left and got into the patrol car. "I need to look into that woman's background. We made her way too nervous. Something's up with her."

Kai looked around the area for bystanders. "I have to agree. Her mistakes make her look suspicious as far as I'm concerned. I'm curious what you might find out about her, so keep me posted.

Rafe pulled out of the parking lot. "Something is definitely up with her. It just isn't sitting right with me. The fact that there aren't any clues left behind is out of the ordinary. I know of a few vacant cabins up in Ravensville. I'd like to take a look at some of them. Maybe we can find the one where the victim was held before the murder."

"I'll go with you if you want. I'm not sure Nate is going to be up and around this week. He took quite a beating. I've never been around magick or witches, but what Logan was able to do was wild and off the charts. I gather not all witches have the same abilities, since Morgan can't heal like Logan can, but her mother does." Kai raked his hair back with his fingers.

"I know, it's crazy. She healed Nate a while back, when we had to deal with Danteleon on the beach. For some centuries-old reason, he thinks Morgan belongs to him due to some promise hundreds of years ago. Witches and warlocks are a strange bunch, and none have the same abilities." Rafe gave Kai a side glance. "How's Kinsley doing? I still feel awful the way things went down. That's not like me at all."

"She understands that. All of this is new to me with seeing her throw those fireballs. I'm used to shifting and working like that, but magick, that's another thing altogether. How's Destiny handling all of it?"

"Shock would be a good word for her right now. She knows nothing of magick, let alone how shifters work and how we feel toward other pack members. I do know that my feelings for her go deep, and I should have recognized it when she was here a few months ago. I think she and Kinsley have a lot to figure out. I don't want our relationship to interfere with their friendship. That's the last thing I want, but I do think Destiny can help us watch for the tissue samples to make sure none of our own hit her microscope. Someone higher up would be looking into shifters and witches. I know they're aware of us, but they have no idea where to look. I'd like to keep it that way."

* * * * *

Logan woke up sweating and in a panic as he sat up in bed gripping at the sheets. The morning sunshine peeked between the blinds. When he looked around, he realized he was at his mom's apartment, yet the memories of last night exploded in his head. He rubbed his face and eyes, wishing he could blank out those memories. With the help of Rafe and Kai, he was able to shackle Danteleon, then turn him over to his grandfather. Good riddance!

Nate had been injured, and he'd healed him! *Where the hell had that ability come from?* A super-human strength had taken over his muscles last night to allow him to do what needed to be done. Exhaustion still wracked his body.

Logan lay back down with his arm over his eyes, and thoughts of Mandy drifted through his mind. She was his anchor and true mate, and she felt that as deeply as he did. After they had finished in Ravensville last night, he'd teleported to Mandy's room so she could see he was not injured and still alive. As soon as she wrapped her arms around him, her strength coupled with his own, and new inner peace took over. She'd felt it, too. It was as if a protective shield had encircled the two of them.

I love you, too, Logan. Be safe today, babe.

Her response to his thoughts shocked him. Their connection was shocking at times. He needed her now, yet here he lay, alone in bed while she still lived at her mom's house. They hadn't actually discussed moving in together, but he needed her at his side more now than ever before. Whenever she was near, he felt stronger and his mind clearer. Living together would help, and with his work schedule becoming more demanding once he started at the vet's office, their time would be more limited.

If the two of them moved into this apartment and he let his own apartment go, they could save more money. Would Mandy's mom approve of them living together? Neither of them were ready for marriage yet. Logan dreamed of owning a nice home before he married, so he could provide for his wife.

Magick might have its upside, now that he thought about it, but they had no idea of the extent of their abilities. He could add to a home with the snap of his fingers, but he wanted to *earn* a new home for Mandy.

Logan tossed back the sheet and swung his legs out of bed to sit on the edge, resting his elbows on his knees and holding his head. He needed coffee now because today he had to read through the grimoire for answers regarding the future powers he would be obtaining. Powers to protect not only Mandy, but his mother, which was more than his dead-beat father had done for her. His father had control issues where his mom was concerned because he certainly didn't love her anymore.

When he envisioned a future with Mandy, he only saw the white light of love surrounding them. He wanted the same for his mother and now she had it with Nate, if outside interferences would leave them alone. Logan would be her lifetime protector.

He strode down the hall to the kitchen for coffee. *What if he just snapped his fingers for a perfect mug of the steaming energy drink?* And with a snap, he held out his hand and it appeared, smelling delicious.

Then the air shifted, and he froze in place.

The last time he felt that, Dreas appeared, so Logan waited to see if he'd show again.

The old man took shape, wearing the hooded brown robe, and holding his walking stick. "It pleases me to see you getting comfortable with your abilities. And I must say, last night you exceeded my expectations, my son. It eases my mind that Danteleon is back behind bars again."

"You were there last night?"

He nodded. "You needed more strength than you're capable of right now, so I just sent some of mine to you. Well done. In time, you'll be more comfortable with healing others, and it will come easier each time. Nate will be fine."

"Thank you for your help, Dreas."

"You will also learn that all you need to do is mentally connect with me and I'll do what I can. You are studying the grimoire today?"

"I'm heading in to study now. Will you join me?" Logan led the way to the sofa, the ancient book already open on the coffee table.

Dreas sat in the same chair Logan had seen Izzy sit in. "These chairs are quite different from the hard wooden ones of my time."

Logan laughed to himself. The old man might not be so bad after all. He began to skim over the spell pages, memorized the way to protect oneself before a spell and do it properly, and noted that several spells were used for stronger connections when needed. Others required herbs and salt combinations.

Then he came to the section of the first-born sons in every other generation, which had brought him to reading the grimoire in the first place. His first-born grandson would be the next protector. *Will I be ready to teach him?* At that moment, he vowed to make sure that knowledge would not be a surprise, as his was, and he still felt the anger boil inside.

"Do not let that fester as you read son, it will only hinder your learning. Keep in mind that you are not only studying for yourself, but for the protector who follows you."

When Logan met the old man's gaze, he was holding a snifter of bourbon, sipping as he watched Logan study. "You will also learn that just because Danteleon is behind bars, the same threat is not gone. There will be others who take his place. Maybe not for the reason he wanted your mother, but other dangers as well. Always keep your guard up."

Logan hung his head and closed his eyes. "Will it ever stop? Will there forever be threats against our safety?" He straightened and looked at Dreas as he picked up his coffee, wondering if every past Protector questioned their heritage. Logan wondered what life was like for Dreas so many centuries ago. The battles he must have fought, not only for himself, but those he'd guided to learn from him.

Dreas took a long pull on the bourbon and nodded. "There will always be those who think they can rule the world their way. The Protector is the mediator, per se. You will learn. Don't ever give up."

"I will make sure my own grandson will have a forewarning of what is to come and what his future will be."

"Do not be angry that your grandfather did not forewarn you and your mother. This is the way it was meant to be, by word of the elders."

"Is there a hierarchy chart of those higher up?"

Dreas laughed. "In due time, you will learn all you need to know, son. Your grandfather is a good man, and his wife is his strength, as your woman is for you. Fate and the goddess have put you together. Cherish that connection."

"It's all so confusing. I'll do my best to make my grandfather proud." Logan turned a few more delicate pages of parchment, and when he looked toward Dreas, the chair was empty. He'd never felt the old man leave and he found that was strange.

Then he thought back on the idea that fate had brought him and Mandy together. How can the ancestors and goddesses see what the future holds for those in a new time? He couldn't fathom what it might take to make sure certain individuals met each other at a specific time. That was just crazy, yet here he was with Mandy already at his side, agreeing to do whatever was necessary to help him.

The vision of their future certainly wouldn't be without danger, he was sure of it. This book must hold more secrets that he'd not read yet, and he knew the day would be a long one.

(Dear reader, you can go take a break, refill your drink, and come back. There is no Chapter 13, like there is no thirteenth floor at a hotel. Rejoin my characters in Chapter 14.)

Chapter 14

His teacher came and went as he pleased but seemed to provide tutoring and teachings that made sense...sort of.

His phone vibrated and a beautiful picture of Mandy appeared. After swiping his phone, her voice calmed him immediately. "Hey, I'm glad you called."

"Something seemed off on my end and that is my clue that you need me. Are you okay?"

"I'm better now. Just hearing your voice works for me." Should he tell her about Dreas? They'd never shared a word about having ancient advisors. He knew he wasn't the only one since Izzy appeared for his mom. Was it only his family who received visits?

"The same is true for me. We need more time alone before you start at the vet's office. I'll probably never see you after that."

"Let me give him a call and set up a time to be over there, but I'll be reading more of my mom's book if you want to come over after your shift."

"I'm off in a few hours. I'll call before I head that way."

Mandy hung up, and Logan called the vet back to set up a time tomorrow to do a walk-through at the office. The thrill of actually working at a veterinarian's office would accomplish one goal and passing his final exam would be another. Being able to earn enough to buy a ring for Mandy would be his next main objective, yet that thought surprised him. They hadn't known each other very long but their relationship had melded quickly. It seemed they were meant for each other and that thought set his heart at ease.

When she arrived tonight, he wanted her to consider moving to his mom's apartment with him if he gave up his current apartment. He hoped her mother Katie might understand enough to let her daughter move in. Logan would definitely make sure she was protected. At least this apartment had already been warded against outside evil. His current apartment wasn't.

Logan went back to studying the grimoire, and as he turned the pages, information from the past made its way into his mind faster than he could comprehend. As he read, he could swear the ancestors were speaking every word to him, as though they all sat around a fire and listened to old stories. They told him of the higher place he would eventually be among the witch community and the Witches Council. His opinion would one day be highly respected. They also spoke of a woman who would always be at his side to assist with his powers and strength. He got so wrapped up in the information that his cell phone startled him when Mandy called back.

"Hi, hon. I was pretty into the reading here. Wow. Wait until I share it with you."

"I can be there right now if I teleport from my room."

"I would feel better if you did that instead of driving. I know he isn't a threat anymore, but I don't want to take any chances. I'll get cleaned up. Give me a few minutes."

Logan set his phone down and realized he hadn't eaten anything today. He went into the bathroom to brush his teeth and shave before

Mandy arrived, which would only give him a minute or two. When he looked in the mirror, he couldn't believe it was himself he saw. His shoulders were broader with more muscle than he'd had only yesterday, his cheekbones appeared more prominent, as well as his jawline.

He blinked a few times, but his appearance stayed the same. Did last night's ordeal have this much of a change to his body? Wanting to ignore it all, he grabbed his toothbrush and set about his clean-up.

"Hello?"

He heard Mandy call out from the kitchen. "Grab a beer. I'll be right out." Logan finished, raked his fingers through his hair, and pulled on a clean tee shirt on his way to the kitchen. Peace surrounded him when he saw her, long blonde hair hung down her back, and when she looked up at him, he got lost in her blue eyes.

Mandy had opened the fridge. "I'll take one, too."

He took the beer from her as she looked him over, from his bare feet to the top of his head and smiled.

"What?"

"You clean up pretty damn good, handsome. I like it." Mandy stood on her toes and kissed him then popped open her beer.

"Do I look different than yesterday?" Logan held out his arms and tipped his head to the side, teasing her, not sure she actually noticed the change in him.

She smiled. "If you were any hotter, I'd be turning on the AC in here. Whatever caused this..." She circled a finger to include his head and shoulders. "...keep it up, it's working. I'll try not to jump your bones today. After all, we are in your mom's place." Then she trailed a manicured finger along his jawline and turned to walk toward the sofa.

Her nearness sparked a need along his muscles that made it hard to breathe. He knew he was blessed by the goddess to pair him with a woman like Mandy, a gorgeous blonde, built, and smart.

He set his beer on the end table by the opened grimoire. "I think it's the magick. This is crazy. Last night during that huge fight, energy moved through my muscles that I've never felt before. It's insane. And when I touched Nate to heal his wounds, the static electricity about burned my fingers, but I knew I couldn't stop midway through healing him. Again, something I didn't realize I could do."

Logan sat on the sofa, held out both of his hands and turned them over as though he'd never noticed his fingers before. He couldn't tell Mandy that Nate had shifted and couldn't shift back until he did the healing. Maybe she had no idea who was a shifter and who wasn't, so for now, he kept that to himself. "I don't know if I want to continue doing the training with Jadis for this Protector stuff."

"I don't think you have a choice after what you told me your grandfather said. The abilities are passed down to the chosen few, and...*you* have been chosen. The Protector to follow in your footsteps has already been chosen, he just isn't here yet." She sat back to cuddle beneath his arm that draped over her shoulders and threaded her small fingers through his. "You *are* something special, and like it or not, you can't back out. We will deal with this one day at a time. I'm here for you. It's weird to think that if we have a future together, one of our children will carry the seed to be the next protector."

His gaze caressed her face and shapely lips that he longed to kiss, but instead, placed a kiss on her nose. "That's a lot to be responsible for. The goddess must know something we don't. Speaking of them knowing more than we do, I need to tell you something, and I don't want you thinking I'm nuts." He proceeded to tell her about the visits from Dreas and all that he'd told him about his new position.

Mandy looked up at him with her blue eyes...eyes that always distracted him. "With the abilities we have, and those we've not discovered yet, how can I think anything you say will be crazy? But I've never had such a visitor. So again, you must be special. Just accept it and when tasks, or missions, come up, I will help you deal with them as best I can."

Logan thought about her words and her unspoken promise. If they stuck together, she would help him accomplish whatever came along. "He said you were my power mate, so he knows who you are. That is just creepy. What if they give me a mission I can't accomplish? I don't deal with failure very well."

"Last night was a great example. You accomplished your mission and did what they asked."

He stared at the ceiling for a moment. "I don't know. While I read today, it was as if the ancient ancestors all sat here in this room with me and I absorbed everything they said. I heard their words as I read." He took a long drink, still astounded that it seemed so real as he read the grimoire.

"Maybe we should go to the restaurant. I think you need to eat something."

"If we have abilities, shouldn't we be able to conjure our own meal with the wave of our hand? I've never seen you do magick. We've never gotten into this until recently and I have no idea what type of powers *you* have."

Mandy set down her drink, shook out her hands and snapped her fingers. On each palm sat a plate filled with Cajun seasoned prawns on a bed of buttered angel hair pasta.

"Damn, woman! I just might keep you around!"

"I guess we can eat here tonight. I hope this is something you like."

He took the plate she offered, complete with silverware. "It smells delicious." Logan's stomach growled as he turned on a movie for them, and they ate in silence as he enjoyed every buttery bite. "The seasoning is perfect on the prawns."

After they'd finished and she snapped away the dishes, Logan grabbed them two more beers. "I'm thinking of moving here into mom's apartment. She said she's not getting rid of it even though she lives at Nate's now. It'll save me money and I'll get out of my apartment. We can start saving money for our future, but...I'd be lonely here alone. So, what do you think about moving in? Would your mom have a fit about that?"

Mandy smiled with mischief in her eyes. "She's asked me more than once if I was going to move in with you at some point. Maybe she's got a boyfriend I don't know about and I'm in the way. I'll talk to her again. It would allow us to save some money."

Logan had already envisioned them living here so he looked forward to the future. "I called the vet and have to stop by there tomorrow to look around. My dream is finally coming true. Healing animals is all I've ever wanted to do. I should hear soon on a date for my exam and then it's all final. I'll be a doctor!" He squeezed her fingers that threaded through his. Now wasn't the time to discuss an engagement, but he knew they were destined to be married. It sounded to him that she felt the same way about their future.

Tonight, they would enjoy what little time they had together. He loved that she talked about the future protector being their grandson.

* * * * *

Kai was anxious to get back to Kinsley after returning from the morgue so he could check in with Kinsley. Rafe parked the patrol car behind the cabins where he and Destiny rented. When he and Rafe walked around back, the girls were sitting on Destiny's back porch. As soon as his gaze connected with Kinsley's, Kai's stomach flipped. Uncertainty poured from her eyes, and he could feel something was off. He prayed it wasn't their relationship.

Kinsley pulled her feet from the railing and sat forward in her chair. "That didn't take long. I hope Dr. Grissom could give you two some news."

Kai leaned against the outside corner of the porch post. "Not as much as we would have liked to hear."

Rafe put a foot on the top step of the porch. "Keep an eye on that stingray report. News of us discovering another body could make the perps nervous enough to make a few phone calls."

"I will. I think you're right. I'm sure it'll be all over the news tonight. I'll check the readout when I get over there."

Kinsley stood up and her vanilla scent drifted to Kai. He squeezed the railing to stop from pulling Kinsley over it and taking her next door. "I'll walk over with you. Then I need to head home and to the office. We've got a chamber networking 'meet-and-greet' tomorrow night, and I need to make sure everything is going as planned. You two should stop in. Maybe keep an eye on a suspect or two."

Rafe nodded and looked at Kai. "I think we could do that. Nate could join us with Morgan."

Destiny stood up and Kinsley hugged her. "We'll have lunch before you have to head back to Portland. Don't forget."

"Sounds like a deal. I'll be in touch."

Kinsley joined Kai as Rafe sat down in the chair next to Destiny. Kai walked beside Kinsley toward his cabin, wanting to take her hand or put his arm around her, but didn't, and they went inside. She placed her hands on the back of a kitchen chair. "I can't stay long. I really need to be at the office."

"I know. You have a job that needs you. I'm glad you're busy. Will I see you later?" Kai leaned on the back of another chair, hoping she wouldn't blow him off. He wanted time alone with her when he wasn't exhausted so they could talk, but he didn't foresee that happening in the near future.

Her eyes said more than her words could and he read right into them, wishing the world could just be blocked out for twenty-four hours. This isn't the way he wanted to restart their relationship, but her eyes held a promise.

"I'll know more once I get to the office and see how much still needs to be done for the meet-and-greet. My assistant is usually good at handling all the details. I'll call you later?"

He stood and stepped over to her, taking her face in his hands. He met her hungry gaze that matched his own. The pull she had on his emotions was too strong. The love he had for her made his chest ache with a need to take her as his true mate, but again, now wasn't the right time.

Unable to resist her any longer, he took her mouth in a desperate kiss that melded them together. She kissed him back as her arms went around him. A passion like he'd never felt before engulfed him, and he didn't want to let go of her.

Kinsley pulled from the kiss and looked up at him, her lips glistening from their kiss. No words needed to be said about how they felt. At that moment, he was eighteen again and in love, falling hard.

"I'll call you tonight when I get home from the office. It will give us both time to think. I have a lot to do at work." She reached for his hands and squeezed them. "I'm going to teleport home. I'll talk to you later. Don't be shocked...because I'm going to disappear into thin air. You've not seen that yet." She gave a short laugh.

He felt a tingle as she let his hands drop and blew him a kiss.

And disappeared.

Kai had to blink a few times and look around the cabin to be sure she was gone. *Will I ever get used to her magick world?* Stunned, he went straight for the bourbon bottle and drank a shot. He hoped Kinsley wasn't having second thoughts.

To take his mind off of her, he remembered he had to check for pings on the stingray system. If their perps made calls, hopefully they could track them.

* * * * *

Kinsley got home and changed. Thankfully, Angela was working at her shop, so she didn't have to explain why she'd been gone for two days, but at some point, she'd have to tell her what was going on.

Once at the office, she had worried for nothing. Her assistant, Kristina, had the caterer booked and confirmed, drinks were ordered, there were party bags on the table for the giveaways, and there would be a crowd attending. She loved her business owners in the Pebble Cove Area. This year many of them were doing well so far with the uptick in tourism, and it was only May. Kinsley hoped the murders wouldn't put a damper on people choosing not to visit Pebble Cove. There were also a few new businesses in Ravensville and down in Hag Stone near the Redwood Forest. She had done her job to make sure the new owners knew about the Chamber and its meet- and-greets to get to know other business owners so they could all network together.

There wasn't a thing she had to do to prepare as her assistant had done it all, as she usually did. Kristina was her right hand when it came to gatherings. Kinsley could relax at the event and mill around the crowd, maybe introduce the newest members. What a relief to not worry any more.

Kristina had said goodbye, then locked the door on her way out, and Kinsley finished a report on the computer. Her phone vibrated and Angela's face smiled at her. "Hi, chickie, what's up?"

"I'm home making dinner and wondered how much to make. No pressure if you have other plans."

"You're so sweet. Sure, I'll be there. Maybe there will be three for dinner. I'm not sure yet."

"Three?" Her quizzical voice had a snicker in it.

"I'm not getting into that on the phone. I should be home in twenty minutes. Thanks!" Kinsley ended the call and sat there. Should she call Kai? Would he come to dinner? She tapped her pen too many times. After rolling her eyes, she composed a text to him about coming for dinner with her and Angela at her place and hit send.

Now she waited.

Was he near his phone?

Was he at the station with Rafe?

Would he care enough to answer her text?

Beepy tones let her know he was responding. "I don't know where you live, but I'd love to come spend a quiet night for dinner with two beautiful women."

Her stomach suddenly filled with butterflies at the thought of being close to him another night. She sent him directions and the time. Now she just had to not act like a teenager waiting for her first date. Kinsley completed her reports and got them filed. The office ran just fine without her here for a day or two. She needed to stop worrying.

Back at her home, the smells wafting into the garage informed her how hungry she was. In the kitchen, Angela was cooking away as she always did, her long auburn hair piled on her head in a ponytail twist to keep it out of the food. Her apron always made Kinsley laugh. On the front it said *'if the cook can't make it right, magick will!'*.

"I don't think there is anything you can't prepare, Angie. Look at this spread! I see buttered angel hair pasta with black olives and parsley, blackened prawns, and your amazing garlic bread." Kinsley turned to the table thinking she could help set it, but Angela already had it complete with wine and glasses.

"I'll leave the food in the pots until our guest of honor arrives. Who am I having the honor to meet this evening? I know Destiny is in town."

"Nope. He's an investigator who is helping Rafe at the station. Talking about murders at dinner might be out of the question. I don't think he can say anything." Kinsley peeked over her shoulder. "And no, you don't get to know his name early. He'll be here in ten minutes. He isn't a warlock, so we have to be on our best behavior."

Angela laughed. "Now you're asking for the moon. You know I'm not good at hiding things, especially not in my own home, but I'll do my best." She stepped closer. "Is he hot?"

Now it was Kinsley's turn to laugh. "I think he's good looking." She shrugged a shoulder and headed upstairs.

Angela yelled up after her. "Gibbs is not happy with you! Just so you know!" More laughing came from the kitchen.

Kinsley changed into a light sweater and jean leggings as she looked around for him.

Gibbs had made himself comfortable at the bottom end corner of her bed. "I'm just sayin'....you could have called Angela to let me know that you'd be gone for a few days. But nooooo. You left me hanging like a piece of yesterday's laundry, you know."

She leaned down and lightly rub beneath his chin. "I would never treat you that way, Gibbsy. Not on purpose and not without a good reason. Besides, you *did* show up at the cabins, so stop whining."

"You shacking up with some guy isn't a good reason for me to show up? I had to!"

"We were not shacking up!"

His little body rolled onto his back with his feet twitching in the air because he laughed so hard.

"You just stop that right now. You can come meet him downstairs if you can behave this evening."

"I'll spy first before I let him see me. You know that."

Kinsley rolled her eyes. "Oh, my word. I'm leaving. I guess we might see you later then?"

"I doubt he'll notice anything except your ass, if you're wearing those pants. Really, Kins?"

She spun around and gasped at his comment. "You can stay up here, or go outside the back way, and avoid all of us."

Gibs got onto all fours and ran around the bed. "And miss the entertainment of him not taking his eye off your ass long enough to eat. Bets are on!"

"I'll be downstairs. He'll be here shortly, and you better behave, mister!" She made her way downstairs, totally unsure of the antics that Gibbs would put her through tonight.

Chapter 15

Kinsley got down to the kitchen as Kai knocked on the door. She first turned to see if Gibbs had made his way down the stairs yet but didn't see him. When she opened the door for Kai, she wasn't prepared for her reaction to seeing how icy blue his eyes were tonight, but his shirt helped make them more blue. She loved them the most, and it was like they could see right into her mind...and read it, no less.

Kai stepped in and she showed him into the kitchen to meet Angela. "The food smells amazing. Better than any restaurant! Is this the gorgeous chef?"

"Angela, meet Kai. He's the investigator helping Rafe at the station on the murders."

Angela's mouth dropped open and she couldn't pull her gaze away from Kai's eyes. She had a glass in her hand and as it slipped from her fingers, Kai caught it before it crashed to the floor. "Oh, my goddess, you saved me from a mess. I'm sorry."

"I caught it. Nothing to be sorry for." He held it out for her to take and she had to look up at him again with her dreamy eyes.

Kinsley could only laugh at her reaction. "Angela...I can help you with the main dishes."

"Of course. Sorry." She turned back to pour the pasta into a bowl and handed it to Kinsley. "I'll get the prawns and the bread. Kai, thank you for joining us."

The three of them sat, Kinsley poured the wine for her and Angela. She'd also poured Kai a snifter of bourbon. As they talked, Kinsley dished up a bit of pasta with several prawns for Kai, then some for her and Angela.

"You have a beautiful home, Kins. I love that ancient iron gate and wrought iron fencing at your driveway. The view of the ocean is nice from up here, and even with a fire pit."

Angela twirled her pasta then stabbed a piece of prawn. "That's where we party with our friends. We can watch the sun set and the moon rise. When the sky is clear, the stars are so bright in the night sky."

"Maybe we can experience that later since we might see the stars tonight. The seasoning on this pasta goes well with the grilled prawns. Thank you. Cheers to your cooking talents." Kai finished his dinner first and sipped his bourbon.

Their conversation stayed light. Kinsley was glad they didn't discuss the murders. She didn't want to create any sadness tonight. She answered Angela's questions about her past with Kai and was happy that they'd found each other again.

Angela held up her wine glass. "Here's to both of you working out any differences. May fate shine a loving light your way."

Kai looked at Kinsley, but she looked away before he could see the need within her soul. Being near him sent a heat through her body that only Kai could create. She wanted them to get comfortable and so far, it seemed they walked on eggshells around each other. *Is it because I don't trust that he'll stick around when the investigation is over?* "How sweet, Angela. Thank you. She moved in with me a few years ago. It's helped with the payments and gives Angela a place to call home. She loves her garden outside."

Kai's gaze darted to the door leading out to the screened porch. "Did I just see a ferret come inside?"

Kinsley choked on her wine. *Shit!*

Angela saved her. "Yes it was. He's been our pet for a while now. His little door allows him to come and go."

Gibbs chose that moment to peek his little head over the back of the sofa, then climbed up and sat very still as he watched Kai. His head tipped from one side to the other and made direct eye contact with Kai.

Kai tipped his head to the side, making fun of the ferret.

Kinsley hoped Gibbs would behave as she scowled and shook her head at his behavior.

Then Gibbs scampered off the sofa, over to Kinsley's chair and up onto her shoulder. He nuzzled toward her ear. "I think you need to take him up to your room. I promise I'll stay out."

Instantly, her cheeks heated.

Kai's laugh sounded warm and deep. "Tell me I didn't just hear him speak to you! But that shouldn't be a surprise after yesterday."

Angela looked from Kai to Kinsley and nodded her head. "That you did, sir! He's more like her protector, so you should be on your best behavior."

Kinsley gave Angela a wide-eyed look but had to laugh along with her.

Gibbs peer over at Kai, then looked at Kinsley. "I like him better, but he better be good to you. Nice to meet you, sir." Gibbs gave a salute with his tiny paw, scurried to the floor, and scampered outside through his little door.

"Why do I feel like I'm dreaming? Animals can't talk. Then again, the past few days have seemed unreal."

Kinsley reached toward Kai and laid her fingers on his forearm. She loved the way he folded the long sleeves of his dress shirt over his arms. "Welcome to *my* world. I'm glad we got to have time together tonight."

Angela got up and started clearing the table. "You two take your drinks outside. You have a lot to discuss. I'll have this mess cleaned up in a flash."

With a raised brow, Kai glanced at Kinsley. "Does she mean with magick?"

Kinsley laughed. "Let's just go outside! I don't even want to talk about *her* magick. Thanks, Angela, you're a doll." Kinsley emptied the wine into her glass, made sure Kai had a refill, and led the way out to their fire pit. Her insides were flipping like fish out of water and her emotions were in turmoil. The familiar feeling of being with Kai again made her want to fall in love all over again, but the walls around her heart were high because of him. She truly hadn't trusted anyone since they parted years ago. "I love that the days are getting longer. We're in time for the sun to set. The colors are beautiful from out here."

Kai pulled an Adirondack chair closer to Kinsley and sat down. "This is a gorgeous view. It makes me happy that you live in such a beautiful home, Kins."

"We love it. We spend most evenings out here where it's peaceful, away from the city enough that we don't hear traffic. The woods over there at the edge of my property line are perfect for shifters who want to snoop around. My property has motion detectors and camera surveillance, so we feel safe. It's come in handy more than once."

"The other day, you said the cabin property was warded. I don't really understand that, sorry."

She realized he had no clue that magick was real. "As a coven, our witch community gets together specific salts and herbs, talismans, and stuff, and we place a spell on the property to keep evil out. Each of our personal and business properties are also warded. If the evil is demonic, we use crushed thorns to add more strength. Evil can be at the edge but can't get past the protective barrier."

He reached over to take her hand which rested on the chair arm, and she threaded her small fingers with his. "That makes me feel better, knowing the evil we ran into the other night. I'd hate to think you would run into that thing out here on your property."

Just his touch made her heart tighten as she wished for more between them. She glanced over at him. "Well, he approached me at one point when I was in the basement of the chamber building. He hid in the corner and threatened me from the darkness. That area has since been warded so that he can't get down there any longer."

Kai just shook his head and took a drink from his glass. "Rafe has told me a bit about this guy. I saw first-hand how nasty he can be. Thanks to Logan, his grandfather was able to get him into some sort of lockdown, right? As a shifter, the magickal world shouldn't surprise me, yet it does, that it even exists. I know that when our shifter transformation happens, it's a shock to mortals like Destiny who might witness that. How is she handling everything?"

"It was a shock, I won't lie. Witches just don't exist as far as the mortal world knows. That's why she will play an important part in watching to make sure none of our DNA crosses her desk for shifters or witches. I think she understands the abnormalities, but if we can somehow get our blood and tissue samples for her, she'll see exactly what to look for."

"The government would have a hundred agents crawling all over this place if they got word of even one individual with the wrong DNA."

His thumb caressed the back of her hand, and memories from their teen years drifted through her mind of so many other times he had softly touched her.

"Kins, I have no idea how long I'll be on this case with Rafe, or be in Pebble Cove, but I don't have a permanent place I stay either, due to traveling so often. It's just easier to use my parents' home as a base when I need down time."

"That's quite a trip to go back east just for a home base. I'm glad I settled here. I love this community." Dare she approach the subject of him leaving one day? *But I have to know what his plans are!* "I'm sure Jennie would let you stay at the cabins for as long as you like." She looked out over the ocean with the pinks and oranges on the horizon as dusk settled in. Once the sun set, the darkness came in fast, but the moon overhead reflected off the waves and caught her attention. Old memories of their private times stirred Kinsley's passion, and she realized how much she'd missed his touch.

"That's what I've done for the past year or so; just stay in cabins or hotels wherever my jobs take me. This community seems close knit for the most part. There are a few strange people and business names, I won't lie." Kai gently squeezed her hand, and she met his gaze.

"Kins...I have to bring this up so we can begin to move forward at some point. I want us to make a new start. When you left for college and I didn't hear from you, I assumed you wanted to go your separate way. The last thing I wanted was to hold you back, so I joined the military, hoping it would occupy my thoughts and not dwell on missing *you* so much. Since I thought you were moving on, I didn't want to call and have you think I was stalking you at college."

She had to lean forward at his admission and nearly dropped her wine glass. He didn't look away or try to avoid going deeper with this conversation. "All this time...I thought *you* weren't interested, which angered me. As time went by, I missed you more. The guys I dated couldn't get me to commit because my heart had built a wall to keep them all away from me. Rafe is the only one who has put up with me not committing. For three years he's waited for me to move into his place and make a commitment to our relationship, which I could never do." He blurred through the tears that welled in her eyes, as she mourned over the time they'd lost not being together.

When a tear rolled down her cheek, he reached up to wipe it away with this thumb, and she leaned into the palm of his hand to enjoy his touch. "How can I make this better for us, Kins? Because I don't want to lose you again." He tugged on her hand. "Come over here."

Kinsley set her glass on the side table, and he pulled her onto his lap. His strong arms embraced her and held her tight as she put her legs over the side of the chair. Because the chair leaned back just enough, she cuddled into his shoulder and neck. His cologne wrapped around her like a protective shawl and set her mind on a path with a future.

Her hand moved up the side of his neck and a pulse beat against her fingers as they sat quietly, listening to the waves. So many thoughts bombarded her, warning her not to fall again. At some point, she would have to trust him and give him one more chance, but could she let the walls down and try?

He brushed a strand of hair from her cheek. "I still love you, Kins. That has only grown over the years of trying to find you. I did call your cell number, but was told it wasn't your number any more. The person I talked to had no idea who you were or how I could reach you. So, I assumed you'd changed numbers on purpose to lose me. I did check the internet and found you at the Chamber here. Since I wasn't sure if you wanted to see me again, I never called the office."

His warm hand caressed her thigh as he held her. "When I saw you in the Dragon's Lair that day, and you met my gaze in the mirror, I knew those eyes only belonged to one person. I wanted to throw you over my shoulder, carry you back to my room, and never let go of you." His fingers turned her face up to look at him. "Is any of this soaking in to your heart? I need you back, Kins."

When his mouth took hers, the deep, passionate kiss told her how much he still cared. Hunger was in every swipe of his tongue against hers. Her fingers threaded through his silky blonde hair, and she kissed him back, never wanting to let go. His hand cradled her head, and his tongue fought with hers, desperate to get the message to her heart. She had to start somewhere by letting the walls down.

He pulled from the kiss, closed his eyes and held his forehead to hers. "God, I need you. Don't shut me out again."

Her nails pressed into his scalp, and she pulled him closer, if that were possible. "I've been mad at you for too long. Too many misunderstandings between us haven't helped. I have to put myself out there and risk another broken heart if this is going to work."

He pulled back to look at her. "I don't plan on breaking your heart, babe. Are you saying that you're willing to try? Because I am."

"Yes." The tears came again as she gave her heart permission to open one more time. "Don't break my heart again. I can't take one more time."

Kai softly kissed her lips. "I promise not to break your heart again. Please make sure to let me know if you think I'm drifting away, because it won't be intentional. It'll likely be work related, but you are who I want for the rest of my life."

Elation soared and her heart swelled. "I don't mean to cry like a baby. I'm sorry." She kissed *him* this time, her tongue searching for his and his arms wrapped around her tighter. His response was the promise she wanted for them to move forward. She thanked the goddess for bringing Kai back to her. Being in his arms again brought back the memories of feeling secure and loved. Her hand cupped his jawline as she leaned back to look at him.

"Uumm...I hate to interrupt, but the crickets just told me things were getting hot over here, so I came to see what's up."

Kinsley gasped as she looked around to find Gibbs standing on the arm of her other chair with his front paws dangling. "What the hell? Are you always spying on me, Gibbs? Come on!"

"I'm just watching out for your best interests. And I see everything appears to be under control. Carry on!" He jumped off the chair, gave a shrill squeak, and ran toward the house.

Kai laughed. "Will I have to get used to him popping up whenever he chooses?"

She laughed and nodded. "He thinks he takes care of me when I'm the one who takes care of him! But yes, he will always be around when you least expect it."

"If he comes as a part of you, I will take you both. He doesn't have powers, does he? I can lock him out of a room, right?"

"His only ability is in helping my powers be stronger when I need him. And he's always there. But...right now he does sleep by my pillow."

Kai threw his head back and laughed out loud. "Oh, my gawd! I'm not sure I can agree to that!"

"Then we'll have to figure something out because we're a package deal!" Kinsley thought about their future and how long it might be until she would have to break the news to Gibbs.

At that moment, she realized the walls around her heart had begun to crumble; Kai had broken through them. She lifted her head from his shoulder and looked up at him, staring at each other for a moment. "What is there that I need to know if I agree to this *mating ritual?*"

Kai gave her a one-sided sexy grin. "First, we need to be alone. No Gibbs sneaking in on us. He'd likely tear me apart!"

"So...I can't talk you into going up to my room tonight?" Kinsley's eyes widened as she waited for an answer. She could have sworn she heard a growl deep in his chest. "Kai?"

"That was just the inner feral animal in me, pissed that I'm going to say no about mating tonight."

"Or angry that you would go so far to tease me and say no!" Disappointment at not having him in her bed tonight left a hole in her heart.

"Babe, you have no idea how bad I want to take you up that stairway right now...but my cabin will be a safer place for us. When we decide to make it happen, we'll both know it's the right time."

"How can I be upset with that answer. Again, you're such a tease." She pulled him in for another passionate kiss and made sure he understood she was ready to take the next step.

"I need you, Kai, whenever you say it's the right time."

He winked at her. "Then teleport us to my cabin right now!"

"Oh, my goddess!" She wiggled her ass into his hardness for teasing again. *Dare she agree to that?*

* * * * *

Tuesday evening at the local event center in town, Kinsley directed the caterers when they arrived, the drinks were ready, and she was grateful that Kristina had the welcome table ready with the raffle tickets for attendees to purchase. She'd also filled many colorful balloons with helium and three each had been placed on the tall tables for guests to chat around creating a fun environment for everyone to enjoy the evening.

Thirty minutes later, the business owners began showing up and Kinsley greeted them once they'd finished checking in and getting their prize tickets. Suzie Jinx, from *Antiques with Afterlife,* showed up with Katie Parker and her daughter Mandy, from the *Krazy Locals Bar and Grill,* Angela, her house mate and owner of the *Apothecary and Potions Shop*, came in at the same time as Margo from the *Magick Knots Bakery*. The room soon filled with fifty business owners and their associates, all networking and sharing ideas for customer service.

Kinsley joined Morgan and Nate at their table. "I hope you're feeling better, Nate. Thank you for what you did to help Logan. You guys saved us all!"

"I'm doing much better. Morgan has helped a lot, and Logan has checked in on me, too. I think Kai is coming tonight, with Rafe and Destiny. She's not gone back to Portland yet."

Kinsley tried not to let her excitement show where Kai was concerned. She didn't want their relationship so public yet, even though Morgan knew about them. "I had lunch with Destiny today. She's enjoying her time here and getting to know Rafe a little better."

Morgan set her glass of wine on the table. "You'll have to congratulate Logan when you see him. He just joined the vet's office and has his exam date set. Once he passes, he'll be the new veterinarian at that office. He's pretty excited; working with animals is his passion."

"You must be so proud of him. He's following his dream and doing very well." Kinsley chatted but kept an eye on the crowd to watch for Kai. Could they hide their secret looks from everyone tonight? Or should she just not worry and let nature take its course?

A noisy disturbance at the door caught everyone's attention and Kinsley excused herself to find out who had shown up. She saw Suzie Jinx hugging Lona Hexley, one of the witches from their coven. The crowd laughed and cheered, since everyone knew Lona. Whether you were mortal or witch, the biz owners knew how much fun she was to be around.

Tonight, Lona had a crown of flowers in her long wavy blonde hair, tie dyed flowing skirt and a yellow peasant blouse. Kinsley had heard that she was quite the charmer back in her hippy days with her flower-child attitude.

"Kinsley! Come over here and say hi to Lona."

Kinsley received a huge hug from the woman. "Welcome back to town. I heard you've been traveling again. Tell us your adventures."

"Yes, I have. My travel company said I was their top sales rep and sent me on a free cruise of the Greek Islands! How could I say no? And let me tell you, those handsome Greeks know how to show a woman the town! Their sexy accent sends you over the top!"

Lona had everyone in stitches. Suzie leaned in so the mortals couldn't hear. "More likely, she tried to teleport to a Greek restaurant, ended up in Greece, and forgot her spell to teleport back home! Don't let her kid you about some free trip!"

Lona laughed with all of them and hugged Suzie. "Don't tell everyone my mistakes. You know I try hard with my magick! Not *all* of my spells go haywire."

Kinsley laughed with her friends. "It's good to see you're back. I'm glad your travel agency is doing so well."

Lona stepped closer. "I think the business name makes people call out of curiosity, and then I book them on a trip! Who wouldn't want to call *Hocus Pocus Holidays* and see where we can send them? Because every trip should have a little magick!"

"Lona? Oh, my gawd!" Robae, the owner of *Glimmering Touch Spa*, hugged Lona. "Patrick and I have missed you. Can I book you for your next facial? You've been traveling forever, sweetheart. I've got some new lotions from Angela that are to die for. You must come and try them."

"As a matter of fact, next Tuesday is open."

Robae pulled out his phone and set her appointment.

"Lona, I need to book you as a speaker for our next meet-and-greet! I'll give you a call later." Kinsley spotted Kai with Rafe and Destiny. The guys seemed to be watching Lance, the owner of *Deadly Cuts Meat Shop*, and how he interacted with the other business owners. She was curious to hear what they thought.

Lona held up her wine glass toward Kinsley. "I would love to talk about travel and tourism here. I think this year will be fabulous. People want to get out and see the sights. They've been kept inside their home for too long after that nasty world-wide virus!"

"I'll check in with you later. You've bought your raffle tickets, right? The drawings will be in thirty minutes."

Kinsley made her way over to Kai as she talked herself down a bit. The way his hair swept over his forehead made him even more handsome. Just being near that man made her giddy. *What the hell?* And tonight, he wore a button-down white shirt, open at the neck, and she could see part of his cougar tattoo on his chest. The way he folded up the long sleeves of his dress shirts made her knees weak.

Kai leaned close when she approached them. "Hey sexy. Your 'meet-and-greet' seems to be well attended. Congratulations."

"Thank you, Kristina did most of the work. She's amazing." Again, his cologne got her mind off track, and she couldn't think. Last night they had seemed to get past a few obstacles that were in the way of their relationship, and now they could move forward...if she stayed out of her own way.

"You're the one who is amazing. Can I buy you another drink?" Kai excused them from the group.

She walked with him to the drink table, where Logan was paying for a beer for him and his new boss. "I hear congratulations are in order with your new job! Your mom is going to miss having you around the coffee shop."

"I'm sure she will, but I'll help out whenever I can. The date for my vet exam is in two weeks."

"You'll pass with flying colors. Now Dr. Clawson can take a break once in a while and not be a workaholic." Kinsley shook hands with the doctor.

"I'm glad Nate talked to me about Logan's interest in working with our office. He'll be the perfect addition."

Kai handed Kinsley her wine glass. "I'm sure he'll be good with the animals in your practice. Not everyone has that special touch." He gave Logan a wink.

"It's my dream job, for sure. I'm going to make the rounds and pass out business cards." Logan reached for his business cards as he and the doctor walked away.

Chapter 16

Kinsley walked toward a tall table that was empty so she and Kai could talk for a bit. It was nice to be out with him. The other women casually watched her with Kai, but she tried to ignore them.

"I love walking behind you. I don't think I've seen you dressed in business attire. I love the pencil skirt and heels. You're killing me, woman."

Her cheeks heated, even in the crowded room. "I'm trying to hold it together tonight. Being around you isn't easy, either. The other women are dying to know who you are!"

He gazed out at the crowd, smiled at a few, then turned his attention back to her. "I've not noticed any of the other women here. They're probably all witches who would turn me into a toad!"

"Oh, my goddess, stop it!" She nearly choked on her wine. "They would surely have better plans than that if they ever got you alone. I can only imagine what they want to do with you!"

Kai leaned in close to tease her with his cologne, she was sure. "But they never will. I only want to be alone with one witch." The sensual look he gave her made her inner muscles clench up on their own. She hated how her body betrayed her around Kai.

Damn if he didn't strike every chord she had.

He looked back at the crowd, nodded to a few. "What are your plans after we finish with clean-up tonight?"

"I don't expect you to help with that!"

"Too late for that thought, but later, I plan to relax at my cabin and think of you. If I could *have* you there...my dreams would come true."

His wink made her think twice. These were the times when she had to forget their past so they could move forward. She already knew he could work her body into a frenzy just by looking at her. The day they showered together told her that and those were memories she would hold onto forever. Would it be so bad to let nature take its course? Then she remembered his shifter side and the real animal she could tame.

"Shit, there is the coroner with his assistant. Let's head toward Rafe and Destiny. I need to speak with Rafe."

Kinsley followed his lead as they made their way through the crowd. Tonight's attendance was over the top. They'd never had this many business people in one room, and she was proud that they all seemed to be passing business cards. Perhaps this year's tourist season would be a success, too.

Once they reached Rafe and Destiny, she chatted with her friend for a few minutes. "I hate to run, but I do need to say a few words and get the raffle started. Good luck to all of you. I'll talk to you when things slow down." She hugged Destiny because she didn't feel that she could hug Kai tonight. Not in front of so many people.

One day, she hoped soon, that they could make their relationship public, and others would be used to seeing them together. Since everyone was used to seeing her with Rafe, and tonight Destiny was here, she didn't want to make waves. Waiting to be with Kai was the right thing to do...like later tonight.

Kinsley got up and thanked them all for coming, then Kristina helped raffle off the donations from several businesses. Receiving gifts from other businesses helped each other, or they donated gift certificates, such as from *Krazy Locals* or lotions from Angela's shop. Again, it was about networking and letting the residents know more about the local businesses.

As Kinsley helped Kristina pack up the leftover food and clean up the table, she saw Kai, Rafe, and Nate tossing plates and glasses into the garbage, rolling up table cloths, and taking down tables and chairs.

She walked over to Morgan and Destiny. "Thank you all for helping. This really was a huge event tonight."

"You know we don't walk away when there are things to be done. We'll help load up your car, too. Go pull it closer to the door for us."

She accepted their offer and pulled her Tahoe around, leaving the back door up so they could load the boxes.

Kai brought out with the first box of food and pushed it into the back. "So...have you made a decision on your evening plans?" He pulled her close and trailed a finger down her throat and over her collarbone, sending excitement through her body.

"You know I'm a pushover. I'll be there but I'm not driving."

"I think I like this teleport thing you do." His kiss was quick, but full of passion and anticipation. "I'll be ready for you."

They walked back to help with more loading. Once things were cleaned up, she flipped off the lights and locked the door.

Angela rode back to the house with her, chatting about new clients she may have gotten this evening, but Kinsley only half listened. "I love these events. It's a great way of sharing ideas for more sales and what draws customers to our locations." When she paused, Kinsley glanced over at her. "You two looked wonderful together. I hope things work out for you. He's pretty sexy, girl."

"He is, isn't he?" Kinsley smiled so big it hurt her cheeks, but she was thrilled that things were moving smoothly. "Hey, who was that hunk I saw *you* talking to?"

"He's an investment advisor from Hag Stone and has a location up in Ravensville. He said he often comes through Pebble Cove; he seems very nice. I got his business card. A lunch date might be in my future!"

"Well good for you! I hope things work out." Kinsley pulled into her garage, and they unloaded. "I'm popping over to Kai's cabin. I'm not sure whether I'll spend the night. I'm sure that's his plan, so if I'm not here in the morning, that's what happened."

"No worries, but thanks for letting me know. I'm really happy for you two. You both deserve to be happy."

Kinsley went upstairs to change but first sent a text to Kai that she'd be there in ten minutes. With her head in the clouds and her heart happy, she changed, grabbed her phone, and nearly stepped on Gibbs as he scampered toward her bed. "You need to make more noise, so I don't kill you some day, dude!"

He curled up near her pillow. "It's nice to see you happy. I mean *truly* happy, because I can sense that you aren't holding back with this guy."

"I don't think it's any of your business, Mr. Nosey Butt."

"Just stating facts, in case you weren't sure. I kind of like him. His eyes are weird though."

"Stop it! His eyes are gorgeous."

Gibbs paused for a moment with his paw on his chin. "And he works out at the gym too much. Don't let him crush you tonight!"

"Oh, my goddess! You stay out of this!" She tucked her phone in her back pocket. "I might be gone all night; in case you're wondering. Good-bye!"

* * * * *

Kai changed into a vee-neck tee shirt, jeans, and tossed his socks in the hamper. His gaze landed on the bed, and he hoped the two of them would be in there later tonight. His inner cougar had been pushed to the limits at the event as soon as he laid eyes on Kinsley's pencil skirt and heels. He barely held it together as he walked behind her when his fingers tingled. He'd stopped a shift just in time. She more than made up for the past memories of their teen years. Now she was filled out in the right places and more beautiful, if that were even possible.

A noise in the kitchen caught his attention, remembering that she was going to *pop* over, and he quietly walked toward the end of the hall. When he saw Kinsley, his breath hitched, and he leaned against the wall to watch her for a moment. His chest tightened at having her so close again.

The years they'd spent apart ate at him.

The misunderstandings between them didn't help, nor worrying that she would think of him as a stalker. She ignited a fire in him from their teen years that still burned hot. If he wasn't careful, he'd shift and take her without notice, and that was the last thing he wanted.

The need she created within his body grew to a fevered pitch and if they didn't settle things soon, he would shift and mate with her without a warning. Last night had nearly undone him, and tonight only made his fire burn brighter at the Chamber event. Her giggle made him smile.

It only took a moment for her to realize that he watched her, when she spun around. "What?"

Damn, she was gorgeous, but he stayed leaning against the doorway to see how long he could hold out. "You're just too cute for your own good."

She slowly walked toward him, teasing with every sway of her hips. It was as though each step she took sent another electrical charge along his nerve endings. Kai had to force himself to stand still and let her come to him.

She did.

Her scent seared through his system like a backdraft, and his jaw tightened at resisting the urge to touch her yet. His animal side wanted out, and his fingers tingled where his claws threatened to pierce his skin.

Take her! His feral instincts wanted to win this game tonight.

She sniffed the air between them, then sniffed again, and closed her eyes as though savoring the memory. A small moan escaped her throat, and after a moment, she looked into his eyes. Emerald pools full of mischief gazed back at him, taunted him, begged him to kiss her.

But he didn't.

Not yet.

A slow deep breath filled his lungs as he tightened the grip on his feral instincts. *Down, boy. You can't take her yet. It's not time.*

She smiled and he remembered they sometimes shared their thoughts. "But you know you want to, don't you? I can see it in your eyes. You're fighting it well." Her lips pouted as she tipped her head higher to meet his six-foot-two gaze, and she took half a step closer, her breasts touching his chest, searing him everywhere their bodies came together.

How could she read his mind? The passion arced between them like white heat sparking back and forth, and he barely held it together. "You're quite the tease, witchy woman."

"Two can play at this game. I learned well from you." She winked, and the sensuous look in her eyes taunted him again. "How long can you hold out, *detective*?"

Fuck!

His teeth bit into his upper lip as she watched him. Every muscle in his body was tight and ready for an assault on her senses. He wanted to wait even longer, but could he?

His jeans got extremely tight, aching for what he'd wanted for the last five days. He knew she already tasted good.

Just give in already!

No! Stay out of it.

She ran a finger lightly down the side of his neck, her touch like a soldering gun against his flesh. His muscles went taut.

Blood pooled in the wrong places.

Her tongue wet her lips and disappeared.

A manicured nail moved over his chest and lightly circled his nipple. His crotch electrified as he sucked in more air.

His gaze never wavered from hers as a green circle surrounded her pupils, and he knew she was getting to her breaking point.

She was stronger than he gave her credit for as he refused to move an inch.

Teasingly, she gently pinched his hardened nipple, watching his reaction. His eyes closed for a moment as he breathed in again, then her firm grip gave a half twist.

That was it!

He bent to her side, grabbed her thighs, and threw her over his shoulder so fast she didn't know what happened.

She screamed out more from the shock, but her arms wrapped around his hips, and her fingers grabbed hold at the front of his jeans.

That nearly undid his resolve as he firmly smacked a full hand to her ass and headed toward the bedroom.

She screamed again.

"I should have done this the first day I saw you, woman. You teased me that day, too! I guess you need to be taught a lesson about being such a tease." He leaned over the bed, and she fell backward, her arms outstretched to catch herself, her long hair spread over the pillows.

"God, I need you." He stared at her as he tried to regain control, wanting to take his time for their first mating but...he wasn't sure he could hold out.

Slowly her foot slid up his inner thigh and higher. "I can see that."

His gaze roamed over her body, enjoying the curves and mounds. "You better be sure this is what you want, because we're not turning back once I get started on you."

She only smiled as she lay still. Then her fingers grasped the waist of her leggings, and she peeled them down her thighs, kicking them to the floor. Only a black, lacey thong remained. Soon, her top flew toward the floor. A black lace bra confined her full breasts, her cleavage begging to be kissed.

He couldn't stop a smile that curved his lips as he unbuttoned his jeans and slid the zipper down. Grasping her ankles, he spread them wide and knelt between her knees. He braced himself on his elbows, and she gently squeezed both of his nipples, tormenting him beyond control as she gave them a half turn.

He scooped her up with a kiss so full of need that he couldn't be gentle about it. A craving needed to be fulfilled. Her legs wrapped around his hips, and he pressed against her, as his tongue ravaged her mouth. Nails raked over his back and her fingers found their way beneath his tee shirt, tugging it higher so their stomachs were skin to skin.

Her fingers tugged at the waist of his jeans until they slid down his thighs.

Passion soared between them as his hands moved down to grip her ass. With that, she had somehow rolled them over for her to be on top. Kinsley pulled from the kiss, nearly tore his shirt trying to get it over his head, then flung it on the floor.

She slowly rocked on his hips, grinding against the length of him as her palms flattened on this stomach and moved up to his chest. Her fingers dug into his pecs, but her eyes never left his. "You are the one who needs a lesson on teasing. You tormented me all evening with your seductive glances and smiles, and I won't even go into the fact that your eyes strip me naked with every look you give me. So don't back down now, because we've already gone too far to stop."

She'd pushed him beyond his limits, and the tips of his claws poked her hips as he held on. Kai pulled his hand away until he regained control.

Then he reached for the back clasp of her bra, undid it, and tossed it aside. Her breasts filled his hands even more than in their teen years, and he pulled her down to make love to her mouth first. She stretched out over his legs, and he slid off her thong.

Moving quickly, he rolled her beneath him, finished off her thong and lifted her knees wide. He stood long enough to push his jeans to the floor. As he admired her nakedness, he knelt between her thighs to let her see himself before he buried it deep inside of her. "You're the only woman who could ever match being my mate. There will never be another."

He scooped her close and breathed in her scent. As slowly as he could, he entered her, watched her eyes for signs of turning back and saw none. She leaned up and pulled him into a kiss as he thrust up inside, their bodies meeting one another as though time stood still. Never had he experienced anything like being with Kinsley. They were as one...for hours, pleasures beyond pleasures. His heart nearly exploded as they came together like no other time ever. She would always be the only one for him.

Kai woke in the middle of the night with his arms still around the woman of his dreams. She looked contented, peaceful, and small whimpers escaped her throat as she slept. He scooped her closer and she repositioned to spoon against him, and he went rigid, wishing they could repeat the night again.

Finally, he understood the strength of mating with the one you love. No other woman had compared to this night. A few other pack members tried to explain it to their single members, but they'd told him he wouldn't understand until he experienced it. All they told him was that he would know when the right mate came along. Now he understood. She made concentrating hard just by being near her. He cupped a breast and went back to sleep.

* * * * *

The warm ocean air blew through the truck window as it sat near the dark deserted beach with only the light of the moon. Waves lapped at the shore with each breath of the ocean. Tension soared with every wave that crashed.

Beads of sweat collected over their forehead.

Making these calls was not a favorite activity.

Not as enjoyable as collecting body organs for others who needed them.

A dial tone.

A raspy voice answered.

"I can't believe you showed your face at a public event! What don't you understand about getting caught? Are you wanting *me* to kill you? It's a good thing your organs are *not* a match for anything. The cops followed you around the entire evening. How asinine are you?"

"Sorry, boss."

"Shut up! The next one better not be a screw up. I have clients waiting for organs. I'll wait for your call. And be fuckin' careful, asshole!"

The phone went dead.

Hopefully, the call was short enough not to be detected.

Another victim had to be chosen, taken without notice, and organs delivered.

Who would be next?

The jockey box opened, and fingers felt around for the envelope. Not enough money yet. More was needed. Quitting wasn't an option.

The water bottle crinkled within trembling fingers.

So thirsty!

Time to start a new search.

Headlights shone over the water as the truck backed up and headed for the main road. A new dumping spot was imminent.

Male or female?

Decisions were never easy.

The headaches didn't help.

Lights from an oncoming car went by as sweaty fingers clenched the steering wheel. I have to drive in the other direction for now.

* * * * *

Logan drove Mandy home from the Chamber event, but first they went into the *Krazy Locals Bar and Grill* to meet her mother, Katie, for a beer before he went back home. Mandy carried in the gift bag she'd won, excited to see what it was.

Her mom had already gotten a table, so he and Mandy sat down, and he took the chair facing the door as he sensed several shifters near the bar. He nodded when they looked his way, hoping to avoid any trouble.

Katie laid her phone on the table. "Beers are on me tonight, kids. They'll be here shortly. The meet-and-greet was packed this month. Do you think you might have new clients coming to the vet's office? I think you did great networking."

"I was excited to be there tonight. Working at the vet's office is my dream job, and it fell into my lap because of Nate. If he would not have said something, Dr. Clawson might have hired someone else."

"Mandy is just getting started on her basic classes at college, so maybe she could take assistant vet classes and work alongside you. I think that would work in your favor for the future."

Mandy reached over and took her mother's hand, her eyes wide and excited. "Mom, that's a great idea!"

Logan loved it. If he one day took over the practice, he and Mandy would be running the place. He raised a brow at her. "Totally up to you, babe, but that would work for us."

Katie tapped her nails on the table. "So, what's in your bag? I can't believe you haven't even peeked at it considering it's from Suzie Jinx and her *Afterlife Antique Shop*."

Mandy set the small bag on the table, sorted through the tissue papers and pulled something out that was wrapped in more tissue paper. She peeled it and turned it over, unwrapping it and a very large antique key landed in her hand, bigger than her palm. "Logan, this is beautiful! Look at all the intricate filigree at the top around the stone."

When Logan lean toward Mandy, the violet Amethyst glowed as though it had a heartbeat while Mandy held it.

Her mother gasped and leaned back in her chair. "Amethysts are known to unlock forbidden knowledge and power." She stared at her daughter and Logan felt the atmosphere change around him. His shoulders tingled.

Logan peered closer. "What kind of lock would that even fit into?"

Katie stared at Logan. "I think you two need to show that to your mother. She has more abilities than I do. Maybe she can figure out a clue, but I don't have a good feeling about that stone."

Logan pulled the tissue papers out of the bag and a small card landed on the table with an old English script. He picked it up and read it to Mandy. *"The past, present, and the future...this key belongs to all three. When the time is right, the lock will find you."*

"Oh, my goddess. That is too spooky. It's beautiful but wrap it back up and put it back in the bag." Katie looked shook by such a message being received for her daughter.

Mandy looked at Logan. He could see curiosity in her eyes but knew she didn't want to discuss it in front of her mother. After nodding his acknowledgement, he handed her the card to keep with the key. She wrapped it back up, placed it inside the other tissue, and returned it to the bag. She set the bag on the table between her and Logan just as their beers arrived.

There wasn't much of a crowd in the bar tonight as Logan drank his beer and looked around. Yet the atmosphere held an electricity for him, letting him know that others here tonight had abilities. Being able to sense them had gotten easier since his training with Jadis and almost came as a foreboding of more trouble. He hoped it wouldn't be tonight. They'd had their share of issues, and he wanted things to calm down a bit.

Since Katie and her friends had warded the bar, evil couldn't get inside so the eerie sense he was getting confused him. His abilities were a blessing yet also a curse!

Chapter 17

Logan still wondered what had stopped his grandparents from alerting him and his mother about their possible magick and to watch for it. His mom had finally let him know when his grandmother passed down the ring from his great-grandfather. One day, his ring would pass to his grandson but seemed like so many years into the future.

What if I'm not here to alert them and who will train him if I'm not around? More questions for Dreas next time he saw the old man. He didn't need something else to worry about at the moment.

The table vibrated and he looked to see whose cell phone lay on the table. His was in his pocket and Mandy had hers in her purse. Katie was on her cell texting and not touching the table, so she had no idea of the vibration.

He turned toward Mandy the same time she looked at him, and he raised a brow. She shook her head. It happened again and she touched the bag. Logan noticed that Katie was still texting and had no idea. He left it at that. "I'll make sure to check with my mom and see if she knows anything. That's kind of creepy."

"Hey mom." Mandy waited for her mom to put her phone down.

"Sorry. I had to finish that text and get it sent." Katie quickly picked up her beer and looked around.

"Texting your boyfriend again?" Mandy teased.

Even in the dimly lit bar, Logan could see her blush. "Nooooo!"

"It's ok mom. You deserve to have someone. You don't need to hide that fact."

Katie looked between the two of them. "He's not my boyfriend."

"Mom, don't stress about it. I just want you to know that I'm fine with that. I'm not going to live at home forever and I don't want you alone if I decide to move out some day."

"I just worry about you being able to afford a place on your own."

Logan thought it was the perfect timing to discuss Mandy's move. "I'm thinking of moving into my mom's old apartment above the bookstore and giving up my apartment to save money. She's at Nate's place now and suggested I move in so it doesn't get run down. There's plenty of room there if Mandy ever wanted to join me. Neither of us would have to pay rent so we could save money that way...if that's alright with you should she decide, at some point, to move out. Just an offer."

Katie looked at both of them. "Is that something you two are ready for?"

Mandy looked at Logan. "It would give us more time to see each other. I'd still work here and help you out, mom, but with Logan working at the vet's office now, we have no idea what type of hours he might work. Plus, his mom will still need help at the coffee shop until she finds someone."

Her mother almost looked relieved that the subject was out in the open. "You two have gotten close since Logan moved here. I'm happy for you two. I know your father would be, too. I do like that the apartment has already been warded, so I know you'll both be safe living there."

"Are you saying...it's okay with you if I move in with Logan?"

Katie reached over and touched Mandy's arm. "It is. I will always worry about you. I've not taught you nearly enough about your abilities." She looked at Logan. "I'm assuming you know what we're talking about?"

He nodded. "Yes, I have abilities, too. We can expand on our powers together. I've been working with an instructor and she's doing a wonderful job helping me learn."

Mandy leaned close to her mom. "Logan is very special. We can't go into it here, but you won't have to worry about me, mom. He'll make sure I'm safe."

"Then I guess I don't have to worry. You two are so cute. Thank you, Logan." Katie held up her empty glass for a refill. "I'm excited for your future. You both know life won't be easy, right? Evil will always be out there searching for us. Promise me you will always pay attention to what's happening around you?"

"I will, mom. I hope you find someone who will be just as special for you."

Katie spotted someone she knew and stood up. "I'll be right back!"

Mandy watched her mom disappear into the crowd. "Well, that went easier than I ever thought it would. I was afraid she would never let me move out. We've never really talked about it much."

Logan took her hand.

The bag vibrated again, and Mandy looked inside. "Well shit!" She looked at Logan. "The stone is still glowing. What the hell?"

He surveyed the room, hoping no one else noticed the issue with the bag. "We need to get the key out of here before someone else senses it. Let's take it to my mom tomorrow and see what she knows."

"I wonder if Suzie Jinx realizes the key has magick? I don't want another beer. I want to know more about this key."

* * * * *

Morgan cuddled with Nate in their double recliner after getting home from the chamber meeting. "I'm glad Kinsley had such a great turnout tonight. I really do enjoy talking with the other business owners, and that's the only time many of us get together. Some have really good customer service ideas."

"Seeing Kinsley and Rafe with different mates tonight was weird. That'll take some getting used to, but I really like Kai. I'm not sure you're aware, but he's a cougar shifter. I think if he stays in Pebble Cove, he'd be a great addition to the pack."

"He's not from here though, right? I guess it would depend on what happens between them in the future. I doubt *she* would move away from here. She loves her job. And the coven needs her!"

"We haven't learned much about Kai. He's mentioned his military background in special forces and that he travels to his assignments all over the country for criminal investigations and murders. Since we aren't close to solving ours, he may be around for the summer. Although I'd hate to think we'd have a killer on the loose for that long."

"Knowing someone is out there murdering people is just creepy." Morgan's phone vibrated. "It's Logan. I wonder what's up? Hey, babe. Did you have fun at your first chamber meeting?"

"I did. Mandy won one of the gift bags and it happens to be from Suzie Jinx's antique shop. We want you to see it. It doesn't appear to be just any old key. I'm going to keep it with me. I don't feel good about Mandy having it at her mom's house right now. I'm staying at your old apartment because it's warded. If it's okay with you, I'm going to give up my apartment and move in here. It'll help me save money."

"I think that's a great idea, Logan. When do you want me to see it?"

"I start work tomorrow so it'll have to be after I get done. Mandy works the dinner hour tomorrow, but I can bring it by so you and Nate can see it. How's Nate feeling, by the way?"

"He's healing well. His pain isn't nearly as bad as the first day he was injured. Just come by for dinner. I'll see you then, hon." Morgan hung up and looked at Nate. "Something isn't right. I'm not sure what, but Logan will be here for dinner tomorrow." She explained about the key and as she did, strange castle images drifted through her mind. Without mentioning the images to Nate, she hoped to figure out their meaning before telling him. Perhaps her mirror would show her more when she scryed the next day.

"I'm glad he called. You've got a good son, babe."

Morgan reached up to pull Nate in for a kiss but instead, he turned her as he pulled her onto his lap and held her. She studied his strong handsome features, and his eyes still drew her attention the most. One was blue and the other light green; they revealed his emotions that tugged at her passionate side. He knew exactly what he did each time he gave her that look, and she melted inside. "If a man could be beautiful, it would be you. I love that you are so easy to look at, but other women also see you the same way."

"Only *you* hold my heart. I'm already mated to the woman I love, so they can try as hard as they want, but none will succeed." He ran a knuckle down her cheek and beneath her jaw to bring her lips to his. The kiss was heated and deep as his fingers wound through her hair to tug at her nape.

He pulled from the kiss to stare into her eyes. "If you planned to put a spell on me tonight, it's working. I'd suggest we get out of this recliner before I break it into pieces trying to retrieve my prize."

Her cheeks heated as she recovered from his hungry kiss. "You're the one who cast the spell. I'm putty in your hands, to do with as you please."

He instantly put down the footrest and carried her down the hall to their wing. "There's more room in our bed and no one within earshot to hear you scream, because…I will make you scream tonight."

His muscular arms held her tight. Morgan knew she had fallen hard for this shifter and counted herself lucky in finding a true love that would last a lifetime.

* * * * *

Logan had left Mandy at her place and taken the key with him. After speaking to his mom, he put his phone down and stared at the glowing bag on the coffee table as it sat next to the open grimoire. How and why had this item been gifted to Mandy? And the eerie message on the old card that dropped from the tissue paper still haunted him. The vibrations they'd both felt at the bar had unnerved them and he had to find out the type of intent this gift held.

The bag vibrated again; the first time it had happened since he'd been back in his mom's apartment. Now the glow that emanated from it called to him to unwrap it, but did he dare? Being alone and unwrapping it didn't bode well with his conscience. Maybe if Dreas were there with him, he'd have some protection against whatever evil the key intended.

A slight electrical current went through the room and the old man appeared in the chair where Izzy had sat. "I felt your uneasiness and knew you might need my assistance. Now I see why." He nodded toward the bag.

"What does that mean? This was a gift to Mandy so it shouldn't have anything to do with me." Logan clenched his jaw, aggravated that he didn't have a clue what the key was for or what it wanted from him.

"Were you with her when she received it?"

"I was. It came from the owner of an antique shop."

Dreas nodded as he combed his gnarled fingers through his salt and pepper beard. "The key has been traveling for hundreds of years. I'm surprised it has taken so long to find her. Then again, she has been well hidden from her ancestors ever since the hanging of Alice Parker in 1692."

Logan thought back on his history class about the Salem witch trials. Then, it didn't mean anything to him, but that piece of information had stuck in his brain.

"Although it was centuries ago, she was chosen much like you were chosen, and you each found your way to one another. Am I right?"

This was almost too much information for Logan to handle. He squeezed his eyes shut for a moment to take it all in...the family ties to the witch hangings, his mother's move to Pebble Cove when they'd never even heard of this place, and the day he first laid eyes on an angel with blonde hair and blue eyes. Yet he didn't remember feeling anything special then.

He slowly opened his eyes and stared at Dreas. "Why is this not written so that someone knew to tell us about this before now?"

His phone vibrated and Mandy's message popped up. *What's going on? I will be there if you need me!*

Logan met Dreas's gaze. "I want her here now so she can hear all of this."

The old man nodded. "As she should be."

Logan texted back for her to teleport to his mom's apartment and within minutes she was in the kitchen. She slowly peered around the corner to see who was with him and he reached out his hand for her. He pulled her toward the couch, and she sat beside him. "This is the old man I was telling you about."

Dreas shifted in his chair and readjusted his robe. "I disagree with your description of me, my son, but it is what it is."

He explained to her what Dreas had told him about her ancestors and the key. Mandy could only stare back at Logan. "Why are we just now finding out about this? It's crazy. My mom didn't hide me from anyone."

"On the contrary, my dear. You were chosen long ago; at the same time Logan was chosen. Your mother may not even know it, but your father certainly did. His death happened as a result of hiding your mother from the evil who searched for the unborn child."

Logan saw the goosebumps cover Mandy's arms as she rubbed them away. "I've never heard of any of this from my mother. Why would she keep it from me?"

Dreas twisted his beard around his fingers as he stared at them for a moment. "I would guess your mother has no clue why her husband was killed, even though she was chosen to carry you. To my knowledge, my ancestors have never visited your mother. Unlike Logan's mom, who has been fortunate enough to have visits from the old woman.

Mandy's head snapped around to look at Logan. "What old woman?"

He looked at Dreas and back at Mandy. "The old woman who used to own the bookstore. Mom thought she was just the ghost around here because she loved the store."

"Izzy had a hard time connecting with your mother and getting her here to Pebble Cove. Your father was in the way. That's now been corrected, even though he tries to get her back.

Which is when you stepped in. I've seen it all happen, my son. You've done very well so far."

Mandy rubbed her hands on her thighs. "This is all a bit much. I've never received a visit or a calling from a ghost."

The old man smiled at her. "What's in the bag?"

She gasped.

Dreas nodded. "Open the wrapping and take out the key."

Logan handed Mandy the glowing bag, curious to learn what else Dreas could tell them. With trembling fingers, she peeled away the tissue paper and the sparkling violet amethyst appeared to have a heartbeat as it lay in Mandy's hand. The ancient brass key had delicate filigree designs that wove around the edges of the stone to hold it in.

Mandy stared at the key as though it were burning her hand. "How did you know it was a key?"

He shook his head. "I know all, my child. I've been around for centuries waiting for both of you."

"Oh my goddess, Logan!"

Dreas laughed. "She's extremely happy about both of you, too. Now...close the grimoire and push the lock together."

Logan did as he asked, careful not to break off any of the parchment pages. Once he pushed the lock into the component, he waited for further instructions.

"This key is to remain with Mandy at all times." Dreas dug around his robe and reached into a pocket. He pulled out a black velvet bag and handed it to her. "Keep the key inside this when it's not being used, as it will have many uses in your future. The velvet has a protective inner shield so others cannot sense its presence."

Mandy closed her eyes and shook her head, then looked at Logan. "How have we both been chosen? None of this makes any sense."

"Touch the gemstone to the face of the lock. First, both of you must have your hand on the key."

She held the key by its barrel and with Logan's hand on hers, the stone touched the lock, and it slowly slid from the component. The cover flew open, and pages fanned open until they stopped in the middle of the book.

Logan peered closer. "The pages are blank."

"Now wave the key across the pages."

As they did that, ancient writing appeared. When Logan read the foreign words, he transcribed the language he'd never seen before, and they revealed a gathering of ancestors who forged a key with an amethyst stone and prayed over it. The story stated that the key would only work for those who were chosen in the future to help them complete the missions to protect the magickal empires. The first grandson and first granddaughter of every other generation of families throughout time would be designated as Protectors should they find their chosen mate.

Logan read these words aloud so Mandy could hear.

"I will leave you both to study what has been revealed to you. I am only a thought away should you need assistance."

Mandy gasped as she watched Dreas disappear, then sat back against the sofa staring at Logan with her hand over her mouth and her face as pale as a ghost. The key lay across the pages Logan had just read.

He scrubbed his face, as if that would make everything go away, but it was of no help. "If we keep studying, as Dreas calls it, maybe we will find out what these missions are, or at least some clue. It doesn't sound like your mom had any idea that you were chosen for anything. It comes from your father's ancestors. This is all too wild."

Logan sat back next to Mandy. "I'm having dinner with mom and Nate tomorrow if there's any way you can change shifts at work so you can have dinner with us. I'm hoping she has some idea of what the hell is going on."

"I can stay tonight and study with you if that's what you think we should do. I can call Kelly. She'll fill in for me tomorrow and I'll take one of her shifts the next day. We have to understand what's in this book."

Logan closed his eyes to shut everything out. "This is blowing my head up. I don't know about you. From what I've already *studied*, nothing has ever been said that I would have a chosen mate, yet Dreas knew. And the key has now revealed hidden writings on the pages."

"Logan…"

He glanced over at her and an aura had formed around her body.

Her eyes opened wide. "What's happening?"

"Do you feel anything or is something changing?"

"It's like a warm, comfortable blanket. Look! The key has stopped glowing."

"And so have you. It's gone. What the hell?" Mandy slid over and he held her tight as she trembled in his arms. She buried her face against his neck, and he rubbed her back. They'd gotten so close these past few months and he'd come to depend on her to be at his side, not only for comfort, but support.

"We'll take one day at a time, but I want you here with me and not at your mom's place. I think we need to explain to her why I want you here. She has a right to know what we've discovered tonight."

She leaned away and they got comfortable side by side. "I never dreamed my family had these kinds of powers, but then we've never been close to my dad's family. I don't really know them. We moved away and came here to Pebble Cove. This place is all I've ever known."

"We'll give ourselves a short break then start studying again. And how was I able to know what that foreign language said?"

"Dreas said the key had unknown powers for us. I hope the book describes what those might be. It sounds like I need to keep the key in my purse all the time. That's just crazy."

"Always keep it in the bag. Dreas said the material would shield the key from outsiders, so does that mean people are looking for the key? My mom has a scrying mirror. Do you know if your mom has one?"

"I've never seen her use one. I have no idea though. What are they for?"

Logan got up to get two more beers and brought them back. "My mom has a psychic ability which she only recently found out about. Her mirror shows her things in the future, and she has to figure out what they mean. Maybe we can watch her use it tomorrow after dinner and see what shows up."

Mandy sighed. "We need to learn what the key means. There must be a reason that you and I are now the keepers of this key. Why is all of this so secret, and only certain individuals are aware of what it can do? If it's to allow us to do special activities, we should know what those are. I hate not knowing what's going on in our own future!"

Chapter 18

Mandy had the key in her purse and Logan carried the family grimoire inside an old computer bag. When he opened the door, something smelled delicious. "Mom, we're here!" He held the door open and didn't go further until he heard her voice. He certainly didn't want to walk in on her and Nate doing the nasty, that was for sure!

"In here, come on in. Nate is out back getting the steaks off the grill." Morgan was plating corn on the cob from the cook pot on her gas stove.

Nate had one of the awesome kitchen stoves with six burners like Logan wanted to have one day. He had lots of plans for a new home once he got a few years of veterinarian work under his belt.

Logan kissed his mom and put the computer bag in the family room for later, and Mandy set her purse next to the bag. He didn't want to show his mom the key until after dinner.

"Hi Mandy! I'm glad you joined us. Can you set this on the table?" She handed Mandy the platter of corn.

"Logan, how was your first day at the vet's office? I bet it was exciting!"

"I loved it, mom. The day went by so fast. Being able to be hands-on with the animals was amazing. Just to watch Dr. Clawson work and diagnose the pets was pretty cool. He's got some of the newest x-ray machines that we didn't even have in college. There are five exam rooms, and an area outside for dogs to play that he boards, and his assistants help with the boarded pets."

Nate came in with a platter of rib steaks and Logan's stomach growled. "Wow, Nate, you guys didn't have to go through so much for dinner! We didn't expect all this."

"Just have a seat and let's enjoy them." Nate set the steaks on the table, kissed Morgan, and grabbed the salt and pepper for the corn.

"Nate, I can't thank you enough for putting in a good word for me with Dr. Clawson. My North American Veterinary Licensing exam is in two weeks. I can't wait to get that behind me."

"Any time, Logan. You deserve a break, and I owe you for healing my leg and shoulder the way you did. I won't ever forget that."

"Then we're even." Logan laughed and enjoyed the steak and corn. Morgan handed him the salad and he filled his bowl.

"So, tell me what's been happening these past twelve hours because I've had visions that I can't even fathom what they might mean." Morgan cut her steak and buttered her corn cob.

Logan finished his corn before he began to tell her bits and pieces of what happened with the key. "First, Dreas showed up before I took the key out of the bag. Mom, it glowed through the tissue paper and the bag! And it vibrated on the table!" He started at the beginning and ended with some details of why the ancestors created the key to begin with. "Supposedly, they attached several powers to the key that can only be activated by the two who have been *chosen*. We had no idea Mandy's father was killed after he hide her mom, while she was carrying Mandy, so that the baby would have a future."

Mandy laid down her napkin. "Mom never stayed in touch with my father's family, so I have no idea who they are other than their last name. They now live up in western Washington. We've lived here in Pebble Cove ever since I was a child. No one has ever contacted us, which I've always thought strange, but mom never talks about them."

Morgan steepled her fingers. "My visions have dealt with dark woods, several people around a fire pit with pots and herbs, and I remember a brilliant purple stone, but why?"

Mandy turned to Logan with wide eyes. "How does she know?"

Logan glanced at his mom. "That's the color of the gemstone inside the key."

His mom looked at Nate, then back to Logan. "I had to go to my mirror this morning before I went to work. For some reason, I couldn't stop thinking about it until I did. That's when I saw a beautiful ancient key with a glowing purple gemstone. That must be it. If it's the same one, it's gorgeous...and more powerful than the two of you can even imagine."

Goosebumps covered Logan's arms.

Nate touched Morgan's arm. "You have to tell them."

Logan looked from Nate to his mother, grabbed Mandy's hand beneath the table, and held it on his thigh. "What else did you see, mom?"

She looked over at Mandy and his heart about snapped in two with worry. "Is your mom seeing anyone right now? I've never heard her mention a guy but...maybe it was just a warning. I couldn't decipher what it meant, but he isn't a nice person."

Mandy squeezed Logan's hand. "I think she might have been texting someone last night. She's never dated that I can remember. I told her that she needs to get out and meet people."

Logan and Mandy helped clear the table so they could have room for the grimoire. Logan put it in the center, with the book locked.

Morgan sat down. "I didn't know it would lock shut like that."

"We didn't either, mom. Dreas showed us."

Mandy opened the velvet bag and carefully handed the key to Morgan so she could see it up close. As soon as her skin touched it, she gasped and dropped the key to look at the raised burns on her fingers.

Nate ran to the sink for a cold cloth, but before he got back, Logan reached for his mom's hand and covered it with his own. As the tingle lessened, he knew he had healed her, but still wondered why it would burn someone else.

Morgan put the cold cloth on her fingers anyway. "Wow. Thank you, hon. You can't even see where the burn was. I didn't see that coming, but obviously, only the two of you can touch the key now that it's been activated."

"What do you mean activated?" Logan didn't remember Dreas saying anything about activating the key.

"Since the key hasn't burned either of you, the key has found its rightful owners...both of you. The magick knows who the *chosen* are. The rightful owners activated the powers, I just don't know what the powers are."

"Let me show you one of the powers." Logan and Mandy together waved the key over the lock, opening it, and the pages began flying until they stopped in the middle where the blank pages were. They waved the key over the parchment and the ancient language flowed until the pages were filled.

"Oh, my goddess." Morgan stared at the parchment.

"It also gave me the ability to read that, mom. It describes the ancestors creating the key over the fire pit and adding the powers, which is what you saw. There's a lot more about Mandy and I coming together." He explained the history of her also being a chosen one on her father's side.

Morgan rubbed her chin. "This explains a few things I saw, just not all of it. The dark forest has me confused but I have a lot coming at me regarding the murders also. It's hard to know sometimes what information should go where, and some of what I see is pretty far-fetched and scary."

Nate adjusted his sitting position. "I know I'm not really a part of this, but what if you take the key to your scrying mirror? You said sometimes it shows you information so it could piece things together." Nate raised a brow.

Morgan moved back from the table with her hands out. "I'm not touching the key again, but you can take it to my mirror in my office!"

"Can we do that, mom? I really want to see what it might show us."

"I'm willing to do that. We have to make a protective circle first, get the salt and candles. I'll get my things. Come on, they're in the office."

Nate grabbed his phone from the counter. "I'll stay out here, babe. I have a few emails I need to answer for Rafe and Kai. Let me know if you need anything in there."

Mandy placed the key in the velvet bag and Logan put the book back in the computer bag, then they met his mom in her office. She had shelves of bottles with herbs and salts, ground up stuff and bags of more herbs.

Morgan sat her mirror on a small table in the center of the office and placed three chairs near the table. Logan watched as she created a salt circle around all of it, stepped inside with them, and closed the circle with salt.

Logan sat still while the two of them set up to scry. White candles also circled them, and she had Mandy light the candles.

"Concentrate on feeling your feet ground, as though roots were going through the floor and think of white light around you for protection. Let me know when you're finished."

A moment later, Mandy touched his thigh. "We're ready, mom."

Morgan removed the black velvet covering from her mirror. "The darkness will clear, and visions will come into view. Some won't make sense, and others will be spot on." Morgan turned the mirror so each of them could see. Logan sat in the middle and they both held onto one end of the key as it began to pulse.

Light stardust swirled through the mirror and a man's face came into view, but he couldn't find what he searched for.

Mandy gasped. "Oh gosh! Dad?"

The man's eyes immediately connected with Mandy, and he spoke very slowly. "My beautiful child. I'm glad you are well, it's good to see. I know you have the key. Beware of its temptations, my child, and use it to ward off the evil. I love you. Look after your mother."

The swirling stardust took him away and Mandy groaned. Logan hated that she didn't get to talk with him longer. They waited. A darker swirl came in with several faces floating around, whispering as they moved around each other.

"That's strange." Morgan reached for the mirror, but Logan stopped her.

"I can understand them, mom. I can only make out a few words, but I hear *'don't'*, *'beware'*, *'be cautious'*, *'look for the light'*."

He groaned when it all faded, and the murmuring stopped. The mirror went black, changed to dark blue, then dark green and the forest came into view. It showed them a path, along the path stood a cabin occupied in the night with smoke from the chimney. Further along the path, they saw an iron door with chains but no lock.

How can we open the door?

Golden eyes blinked twice and disappeared.

Bags of herbs flew from Morgan's shelving and scattered over the floor. White candles from the shelf landed among the herbs. The ceiling lights flashed in Morgan's office and Mandy screamed when the mirror fell over. The flame on each candle got snuffed out.

Logan still held the key with Mandy, but a tug made him grip it tighter. "No, you can't have it!" He checked to be sure Mandy was okay. "Put this back in the bag, then into your pocket.

Morgan looked at both of them. "Oh gosh! I'll get the sage. We each need to take one, light it and let it smolder. Whatever came through the mirror needs to be sent away. Mandy, please open that window so the evil can escape!" Morgan picked up the bags and replaced them on the shelves, grabbed three sage bundles to light and passed them out.

"I'm sorry, mom. I had no idea this might happen."

She handed Logan and Mandy a sage. "Not to worry. Let's just get the saging done. Wave it and blow it into the upper and lower corners." Morgan closed her office door, made sure each bundle smoldered, and they went to the corners, then waved the smoke toward the open window. Suddenly, all of the smoke was sucked from the room and the window slammed down.

"Thank you, goddess!" Morgan sat in a chair and put the sage bundles in a dish. She cut the tips off so she could use the bundles again. Logan swept up the salt and Mandy gathered the candles for Morgan.

"Let's go back to the table."

When Morgan opened the door, Nate was there waiting with open arms. He held her tight and glanced at Logan. "It's okay. She knew what to do. Don't blame yourself, Logan."

Nate just held his mom, and Logan touched her shoulder, glad she had someone to comfort her when she needed it.

"I'm good, honest." She shook out her arms and sat down in the kitchen.

Nate brought over bourbon and small glasses. "For those of you who need some. I take it that wasn't a good scry?"

Morgan held out her glass to Nate. He poured; she drank. "No. I think it was a strong warning that others want the key."

Mandy held out her glass. "Something tried to pull it from our hands."

Logan drank with them, proud that Mandy drank it straight down. "I would never have asked if we knew that would happen."

Nate set down his glass. "It's not the first time evil has shown itself in that mirror. Your mom showed me some of them when they appeared. I won't lie. I know how scary it can be."

"Dreas explained a lot. I'm still not used to him popping in, but I'm getting that...when I need answers to this magick shit, he knows when to stop in."

Morgan tipped her head and gave him a wide-eyed stare with raised brows. "Magick shit?" She rolled her eyes and shook her head.

"I don't know what goes on in *your* head, mom, with being some sort of psychic, but I know what's in my head and that's bad enough. How do I live a normal life? Does evil always play a daily role? Because I didn't sign up for any of this. These last two weeks have been a bit much. I want to pass my exam and not have any interference. So, from now until then, I'll be studying my *class* books. You can keep *your* book here."

Nate put his hand on Logan's shoulder. "That sounds like a good idea, Logan. Clear your head. Get your doctor stuff down pat so we can celebrate when you pass. Dinner is on us, how's that sound?"

Logan really liked Nate. He went out of his way to make life better for those around him, and he was someone he knew would stick up for him no matter what. "I look forward to that. Thanks. I think we need to get going. Oh, by the way, I hope it's fine with you that Mandy moves into your old apartment with me. We can start saving money and I can make sure the key is safe with us. Your place is warded so we're good there. My old apartment isn't."

She got up to hug him and Mandy before they left. "Stay safe. I'm a thought away if you need me. Remember that."

"We have to explain all of this to Mandy's mom. I don't think she has any idea about what we're going through. I'm sure her husband's family has their grimoire."

Morgan paused. "Then if they're studying that, they know Mandy is the *chosen* one on their side. That isn't good. But you wear your amulet, thank the goddess."

Logan pulled Mandy close. "I hope we don't have to worry that they might try to grab her away."

"Keep your senses alert at all times when you're out. Both of you. You'll be protected at my apartment, and the bar, but not walking the street. Be careful. Love you guys."

Logan had more on his mind than he needed now. His exam date was getting close. and he needed to get past that hurdle first. Would Mandy be safe carrying around the key? Granted, her mother's restaurant, bar, and home were warded, but he didn't want her roaming off protected property. There had to be something good in taking on this Protector job that he'd *inherited,* but a head's up would be nice.

Mandy took his hand as he drove. "We'll be okay, babe. We can't live looking over our shoulder all the time. I'll explain all of this to mom when I get home. She needs to be aware of all the history, not to mention who that guy is that my mom was texting."

Logan feared it might be one of her father's relatives who may have discovered where her mother now lived. Then he remembered the way he felt in the bar the other night after the Chamber event. His senses had been on high alert, and he'd assumed it was due to the shifters there. *What if it were someone else I detected?* He hated the fear that seemed to be a cloud over their heads, no matter what they did or where they went.

Mandy squeezed his hand. "Don't take me home tonight. I want to be with you."

Logan nearly drove off the side of the road as he corrected their path away from the graveled edge. "What are you saying? Are you sure this is what you want?"

"I want to be with you tonight. We can just cuddle, and I'll feel safer. I'm not sure I want the key at my mom's place if there's a chance her family might be looking for us."

Logan collected himself and turned his truck around to head back to his mom's apartment. "That makes sense. You're right. Let your mother know your decision so she doesn't worry about you not coming home tonight."

He'd never spent a full night with Mandy since they'd been seeing each other, and his body knotted up just thinking about her in the same bed. Neither of them had ever had sex yet, at least he hadn't, and he doubted Mandy had.

The evening could be an uncomfortable one trying to sleep and not take her tonight. He wanted their first time to be something special, not a rushed situation.

She let go of his hand and scooted to the middle of the seat and placed her hand on his thigh as he drove, her heat penetrating up his thigh. Logan fully doubted that she had any idea how a simple hand on his thigh could cause his body to react the way it was.

Concentrate on driving!

Get her to the apartment safely!

Chapter 19

Rafe's mind still reeled from the whirlwind of his last hour with Destiny. He held her close as they cuddled in her bed at the cabin. How could he have not realized that she was his true mate the first time she visited Pebble Cove?

Her scent alone should have clued him in but at the time, he'd wanted Kinsley so bad. The situation between all of them had worked out for all involved and he glad that fate had intervened.

The angel in his arms had light red hair threaded with gold, soft and straight, which framed a delicate face with blue eyes. Rafe brushed a strand of hair from her cheek.

Her nail trailed over his chest. "I had no idea sex could be so good. I guess I haven't slept with the right man until you. I've never had stars explode in my head, nor had my lungs nearly collapsed."

"Other men have never taken you over the edge? Seriously? A woman should always feel that before a man does, unless they're totally selfish." His cell phone vibrated on the nightstand and Diablo's picture appeared. "I have to take this. He never calls me this late."

Rafe sat up and took the call. "What's up?"

"I need you and the shifters ASAP! A California pack is here in the bar with at least twenty shifters, and fights with our guys are starting. Get as many as you can as soon as you can! They're harassing Steph and my guys aren't taking it well."

"We'll be there soon. Kinsley can get us there!" He ended the call. "Son-of-a-bitch!"

"Babe, what happened?" Destiny sat up and pulled the sheet over herself.

"I'm leader of our shifter pack. I need to call Kai and Nate, and they can call a few other pack members. A California pack is trying to take over the Dragon's Lair down in Hag Stone. I hate to leave you again, but this is major. They tried this a few years ago and a few of their shifters ended up dead. Now, they want Stephanie, Diablo's woman, who helps him at the bar." Rafe put calls out to Kai and Nate and explained what was happening. While he waited for them to get to the cabin, he called a few of his deputies, and the fire station to alert some other pack members. Their loyalty put pack business before anything else.

Rafe had just dressed when a knock on the screen door sounded. He let Kai and Kinsley inside. "I hated to wake you so late. Diablo needs us. The California pack is at it again." He looked from Kai to Kinsley just as Destiny came from the bedroom in a robe, and he scooped her close. "I hate to ask, Kins, but I need you to teleport us to the Dragon's Lair. We don't have time to do the drive."

Kinsley pulled her hair into a ponytail, pulled the scrunchie from her wrist, and wrapped it around her hair. "You know I'll do what I can. Did you ask Nate to bring Morgan? I might need her help."

"I did. He and Morgan are waiting at their place. The deputies and firefighters are meeting there, too." Rafe hugged Destiny. "I need you stay put. I'll be back when we get this thing cleaned up. You would be a beacon to them without any abilities. I'm not taking that chance. I know you're safe here. Please do not leave the property."

Destiny nodded, but he knew she felt helpless.

Kinsley hugged her friend, then held out her palm and Kai placed his hand there. "We're ready when you are, Rafe."

Rafe's hand covered Kai's and he felt the magick tingle as they disappeared and instantly stood in Nate's driveway. A crowd had already gathered, and they appeared ready for anything. His pack knew of the powers the witches held, and tonight wasn't the first time they had assisted his pack during a fight.

Kinsley joined Morgan. "We can each take four at a time, then return for the others until we're all at the bar. Since you've never been there, you'll go with me, Rafe and Kai, so you can see where we're going. That way, you know how to get the next group to that location." She looked at the crowd gathering and knew them all. "We'll get you guys to the parking lot down there, and then you're on your own. Morgan and I will back you up as best we can. Let's go." She held out her palm for Morgan, Kai and Rafe.

Once they had joined in, she squeezed their hands, and they soon stood in the gravel at the

Dragon's Lair. The shouting from the bar drifted out to where Rafe stood with Kai. "Thanks, Kins. I owe you. Get the rest of them here." He nodded to Kai and headed toward the bar. "Let's go see what kind of trouble we can drum up. I think you know what to do."

Before he even reached the door, he sensed trouble. Diablo stood in front of the bar and made Stephanie stay behind it. A few other pack members stood beside Diablo facing the angry mob. "We got here in time for the fun. I doubt we can talk them down, but let's head in for a drink and see what's up."

Rafe went in the door first and all eyes turned to Kai as he followed Rafe in. Kai stood a hair taller than Rafe, but his shoulder span was wider. As Kai walked by the pool table, he grabbed one of the sticks and held it as a weapon on his way to the bar.

Rafe glanced behind him and noticed as a few bikers backed down when they saw Kai, but two burley bikers decided their own fate and approached him and Rafe.

"A ways outta your jurisdiction, aren't you, Sheriff?" The bearded man stood nose to nose with Rafe.

Rafe rolled his shoulders. "You weren't with your pack a few years ago, were you? Or you'd know better than to start trouble in this bar."

Another man yelled at Rafe. "This year, we'll own this bar when we're done tonight!"

Rafe saw Diablo shift next to the mouth biker and his bear claw knocked that shifter across the floor.

The other biker drew back his arm at Rafe, and the pool stick landed upside his head. Instantly, Rafe put the man in head lock and ran him into the edge of the bar, where he landed on the floor. Two of his friends backed away. "Get his ass out of here, now! And if you want to live one more day, get on your bike."

Two other bikers jumped the bar to attack Stephanie and grabbed her around the waist. Rafe laughed to himself as he watched her transform into her grizzly mode. She reached over her head, and her claws picked up her attacker and threw his body over the bar, where his friends caught him. The four shifted into wolves and circled Stephanie.

Rafe glanced at Kai and nodded. He'd seen what Steph could do, and instantly he and Rafe shifted. At the same time, the strangers all transformed. Bears threw wolves over pool tables, wolves fought wolves, and a lone cougar took out two wolves at once.

Rafe saw Nate and the others join them when they arrived and shifted into battle mode. Several ended up outside the bar in the grass and some in the parking lot, knocking over Harleys. He knew Diablo and Stephanie could control the inside, so Kai followed him outside to join in the fighting. Rafe spotted two wolves sitting near the woods, and instantly knew it was Kinsley and Morgan in disguise, patiently waiting for their cue to help. Hopefully, he wouldn't need them.

Another grizz came after Kai and he didn't back down. Kai's cougar stalked around the bear, taunting him. At the same time, one of the wolves near the woods crouched down on all fours, the hair on her back standing straight.

Kins, back off. He can handle this!

She paced.

The bear swiped hard and as his paw missed the cougar and went in front of his body, Kai attacked and chewed into the bear's neck, biting down hard. The grizz landed on his back and rolled over. The cougar refused to let go, and Rafe saw his powerful head give a shake and the bear lay dead. The cougar jumped away limping and bloody but waited to see if the bear would move.

Rafe saw Kinsley change back and she ran toward Kai as he transformed from shifter, his side clawed away and bloody. She motioned for Morgan to join her, and Rafe ran toward Kai but stayed in wolf mode for their protection. With a wave of her hand, Kinsley clothed Kai in a pair of sweat shorts, and Rafe chuckled to himself.

Morgan helped her with Kai's wounds, and soon they had the bleeding stopped. He'd watched Morgan touch Kai's side and as Kinsley held onto Morgan's shoulder, she was able to heal the cuts enough so they wouldn't bleed out.

As Rafe looked around, the crowd had thinned, bikes were gone, and wolves and bears lay dead or badly wounded. He went in to check on Stephanie and Diablo. He and Nate were rounding up the rival pack members and making them pick up their wounded to haul them away.

It took a few hours until they were gone and by that time, Kai came in with Kinsley and Morgan. Nate brushed off a stool for Morgan and she sat beside him. The two women looked around at all the damage to the pool tables, bar chairs, tables and shattered mirrors.

Stephanie took a pool cue and cleared the bar, then set glasses and bourbon out. "Help yourselves. I think we all deserve a shot."

Rafe poured a shot for Kinsley and Kai, while Nate took care of Morgan's glass.

Kinsley nodded at Steph as she waved her hand around. "Would you like some help with putting this place back together?"

Kai leaned toward Rafe and shook his head. "More magick shit?"

Rafe laughed but all of them were in awe as Morgan had replaced all of the broken windows. Then Kinsley pointed at the pool tables and Rafe watched them get replaced with newly felted tables and racked balls. New cues lined the walls, mirrors were replaced and with a wave of her hand, the mess on the floor flew out the doors and disappeared. New tables and chairs were arranged around the bar.

When she'd finished, Kinsley sat next to Kai, and Steph poured her and Morgan another shot.

Kai raised his glass in a toast. "You deserve two for all that work, and…she also disposed of the dead bodies outside into the redwood forest over there!"

Rafe rolled his eyes. "California can worry about those bodies. That area *is* out of my jurisdiction!"

Glad that she could repair the bar for Diablo and Stephanie, Kinsley relaxed. The week had been too much for all of them and so much had happened. She glanced straight ahead, into the mirror where she'd first seen Kai a month ago, and their eyes met again.

His gaze seemed to reach out and claim her, if that were possible. The way his hair swept over his forehead looked like he'd just come in from a windy day instead of a brawl with wolves and bears. She knew that the two of them were meant to be soul mates.

Diablo spoke up as he looked at Kai. "Welcome to the pack, brother! I see you still didn't listen, did you? I take it you didn't leave her alone."

Kinsley leaned back and let out a laugh as she remembered that day Diablo tried to warn him to leave her be. "And I'm the lucky one because he didn't give up on what he wanted." Kinsley pulled Kai close for a kiss.

She knew her heart was now where it should be, and their future would be spent together forever. Kinsley looked over at Rafe and prayed that Destiny would hold on to his heart and be his forever-love, but she knew that fate didn't always play fair.

When a shudder went down her back, she saw something move in the large mirror. A man stood in the dark corner behind her and his aura glowed around him, yet when she spun around to look at him, he was no longer there!

Morgan had spun around at the same time. "You saw him, too!"

"I did!" Kinsley stared at Morgan, then peered into the back corner, but no sign of the stranger lingered. She shook her head at Morgan and turned back to face the mirror. The others had not seen the stranger, only she and Morgan saw him, and an eeriness crept into her brain.

The rest of the night, she caught Morgan also checking the mirror for danger. Danteleon was behind protected bars that stopped his powers, but she knew that eventually, others would take his place. *Why can't our lives just be normal for a few days.*

Hopefully, they will be.

Continued in Book 3

Coastal Midlife Potions

More Information

Watch for more books in the Pebble Cove Series by subscribing to Brandi Wilde's newsletter which you'll find on her website:

https://brandiwildeauthor.com

If you enjoyed this book, please consider leaving a review at your favorite online store, GoodReads.com, or go to Brandi's blog on her website where reviews can be left in the comments section for each book. She truly appreciates all her readers. Be sure to tell your friends about her series.

About the Author

Brandi Wilde lives in the Pacific Northwest with her husband, a retired captain of the area fire department and previous law enforcement officer. She plots her upcoming books about witches, shifters, and demons in locations around the Pacific Northwest. Brandi also writes under the pen name Deanna Jewel. You can visit her website at:

https://DeannaJewelAuthor.com

As Deanna Jewel, she writes historical fiction, time travel romance, contemporary, and paranormal romances.

www.ingramcontent.com/pod-product-compliance
Lightning Source LLC
Chambersburg PA
CBHW030744310726
48969CB00005B/1311